PRAISE FOR THE W9-BTB-954

"Reynolds has created a character whose journey is so genuine that he's worthy of a place alongside Ramona and Joey Pigza on the bookshelves where our most beloved, imperfect characters live."

—*New York Times* on *Ghost*

★"This is raw and lyrical, and as funny as it is heartbreaking. . . . An absolute must-read for anyone who has ever wondered how fast you must be to run away from yourself."

—*Booklist*, starred review of *Ghost*

★"The story of Ghost's evolving relationships with his anger, with his ever-worried mother, with Coach Brody, and with running is a joy to read."

—*Shelf Awareness*, starred review of *Ghost*

★"This 'second leg' of Reynolds's series is as satisfying as its predecessor and a winning story on its own."

—*School Library Journal*, starred review of *Patina*

★"The plot races as fast as the track runners in it. . . . Complete, complex, and sparkling."

—*Booklist*, starred review of *Patina*

★"Reynolds has done an excellent job of providing insights into the life of an African American middle schooler. . . . Humorous and authentic."

—*Horn Book*, starred review of *Patina*

★"Another stellar lap."

—*Kirkus Reviews*, starred review of *Patina*

★"Compulsively readable. . . . Another literary pacesetter that will leave Reynolds's readers wanting more."

—*Kirkus Reviews*, starred review of *Sunny*

★"Reynolds again uses his entrancing grasp of voice to pull readers into the heartbreaking world of the Track series."

—*Booklist*, starred review of *Sunny*

also by **jason reynolds**

When I Was the Greatest

The Boy in the Black Suit

All American Boys

As Brave As You

Long Way Down

For Every One

Look Both Ways

The Track Series:

Ghost

Patina

Sunny

LU

TRACK: BOOK 4

jason **reynolds**

A Caitlyn Dlouhy Book

ATHENEUM BOOKS FOR YOUNG READERS
New York London Toronto Sydney New Delhi

If you purchased this book without a cover, you should be aware that this book is stolen property. It was reported as "unsold and destroyed" to the publisher, and neither the author nor the publisher has received any payment for this "stripped book."

ATHENEUM BOOKS FOR YOUNG READERS
An imprint of Simon & Schuster Children's Publishing Division
1230 Avenue of the Americas, New York, New York 10020

This book is a work of fiction. Any references to historical events, real people, or real places are used fictitiously. Other names, characters, places, and events are products of the author's imagination, and any resemblance to actual events or places or persons, living or dead, is entirely coincidental.

Text copyright © 2018 by Jason Reynolds
Cover illustrations copyright © 2018 by Vanessa Brantley-Newton
All rights reserved, including the right of reproduction in whole or in part in any form.
ATHENEUM BOOKS FOR YOUNG READERS is a registered trademark of Simon & Schuster, Inc. Atheneum logo is a trademark of Simon & Schuster, Inc.

For information about special discounts for bulk purchases, please contact Simon & Schuster Special Sales at 1-866-506-1949 or business@simonandschuster.com.

The Simon & Schuster Speakers Bureau can bring authors to your live event. For more information or to book an event, contact the Simon & Schuster Speakers Bureau at 1-866-248-3049 or visit our website at www.simonspeakers.com.

Also available in an Atheneum Books for Young Readers hardcover edition
Book design by Debra Sfetsios-Conover and Irene Metaxatos
The text for this book was set in ITC Stone Serif Std.
Manufactured in the United States of America
0919 OFF
First Atheneum Books for Young Readers paperback edition October 2019
10 9 8 7 6 5 4 3 2 1
The Library of Congress has cataloged the hardcover edition as follows:
Names: Reynolds, Jason, author.
Title: Lu / Jason Reynolds.
Description: First edition. | New York : Atheneum, [2018] | Series: Track ; 4 | "A Caitlyn Dlouhy Book." | Summary: "Lu knows he can lead Ghost, Patina, Sunny, and the team to victory at the championships, but it might not be as easy as it seems. Suddenly, there are hurdles in Lu's way—literally and not-so-literally—and Lu needs to figure out, fast, what winning the gold really means"—Provided by publisher.
Identifiers: LCCN 2018025798
ISBN 9781481450249 (hc) | ISBN 9781481450256 (pbk) | ISBN 9781481450263 (eBook)
Subjects: | CYAC: Track and field—Fiction. | Conduct of life—Fiction. | Family life—Fiction. | Pregnancy—Fiction. | Albinos and albinism—Fiction. | African Americans—Fiction. | BISAC: JUVENILE FICTION / Sports & Recreation / General. | JUVENILE FICTION / Social Issues / Adolescence. | JUVENILE FICTION / Social Issues / Friendship.
Classification: LCC PZ7.R33593 Lu 2018 | DDC [Fic]—dc23 LC record available at https://lccn.loc.gov/2018025798

for the leaders

1

MY NAME: Lightning

I am

The man.

The guy.

The kid.

The one.

The only.

The Lu. Lucky Lu. Or as I call myself, Lookie Lu. Or as my mom calls me, Lu the Lightning Bolt, because lightning so special it don't never happen the same way or at the same place twice. That's what she says. And I like the nickname, but I don't believe that. Don't believe lightning won't hit the same tree, or the same house, or the same person more than once. I think Mom might've missed on that one. I swear, sometimes she just be talking to be talking. Plus, how would she even know that? I mean, she know a lot of stuff about stuff because she's a mother and mothers gotta know stuff, but the people who went to school for that kind of thing, like weather people and meteorologists (who should be studying meteors and not weather), *they* don't even be knowing (because they should be studying meteors and not weather). Talking about it's a 50 percent chance it might rain. A little. A lot. Today. Or maybe tomorrow. I mean, *come on*. And I'm supposed to just believe lightning don't never strike the same place twice? Ever? *Right*.

You know who really made me know my mother was wrong? Ghost. One time he told me about this guy—name start with a *R*—who holds the world record for getting struck by lightning, not once, not twice, not three times, not FOUR times, not FIVE TIMES, NOT SIX TIMES, but . . . *SEVEN TIMES!* If I was Ray or Ron or whatever his name is (or was, because he *gotta* be dead), I would've stayed in the house after the second one. I mean, what was he thinking? Knowing him (I don't really know him, but I know people like him so that's basically the same thing), *he* was probably listening to a meteorologist. Or my mother, who by the way, when she says the thing about lightning striking, don't even be talking about real lightning. Like electric bolts in the sky? Nah. She just be talking about electric . . . moments . . . in life. And I, clearly, was the most electric-est moment in hers. One in seventeen thousand. Albino. Born with no melanin, which means born with no brown. And honestly, I wasn't supposed to be born at all, because my mom wasn't supposed to be able to have kids. So a two-time special once-in-a-lifetime thing.

Until yesterday.

It was Sunday dinner, which is the same as Monday, Tuesday, Wednesday, Thursday, Friday, and Saturday dinner except Mom always tries something new with the food. And this Sunday my dad, who normally works late, was there at the table with my mom to drop the new news on me.

"We're having another baby." They almost sang it out, like a song hook or something. Like they *one-two-three*'d it and everything.

"You for real?" That's all I could really get out— *let* out—but inside my head was going, *Yo you serious like really for real real talk no jokes stop playing it ain't*

3

funny if you playing wait what nah can't be you really really r e a l l y for real?, stretching my neck trying to see my mother's stomach, even though she was sitting down. Dad was tucking his gold chains in his shirt—he always did that whenever he was eating—then popped me on the arm with the back of his hand. And when I looked at him, wondering what he did that for, he just shook his head real fast like he knew something I ain't know. Like he knew something I ain't want to find out. "Sorry," I yelped. "It's just . . . I can't even tell!"

I pinched and pulled a piece of meat from the turkey wing on my plate, a recipe my mom said she got from Patty's aunt. Tasted pretty good too, even though it seemed weird to just be eating turkey wings without the rest of the turkey. That's what chicken wings are for.

"We're *very* for real." Mom smiled. "We're just about at three months, and they're saying on December sixth you gon' have a little brother or sister." I swear her face was glowing like there were lightbulbs in her cheeks. "That's why I've been more tired than usual, and why I'm sometimes late picking you up at practice. Been a little sick during the day."

"Sick?"

"Yeah, nothing serious. Normal pregnancy stuff. But that part should be almost over." She crossed her fingers. "Oh, and . . . well . . . thank you for *not* being able to tell by looking at me. Trust me, I'll be poking out soon enough. Y'know, it took a while for you to make your presence known too."

"And the boy ain't stopped since," my dad threw in.

"Ain't that the truth." Mom pressed her shirt against her stomach just enough to show a bump no bigger than the kind you get after a Thanksgiving meal. Only difference is it wasn't Thanksgiving, even though . . . turkey. "Anyway, we're telling you now because tomorrow we have a doctor's appointment."

"I'm going?"

"I mean . . . well, we thought about it, but it's your championship week, you know?" She set her fork down. Folded her arms on the table. "You *wanna* go? Or would you rather go to practice?"

Tricky. I definitely wanted to go to the doctor to see what was going on with the baby, but not if they did what I thought they were going to do there.

"Depends. They going to do that thing with the . . ." I balled up my fist and slowly moved it over my stomach to demonstrate how they pull out that machine-thing that turns the baby into a blob of virtual reality with the heartbeat and all that. "And then the baby'll show up on the screen looking like old footage of the moon landing?" A blob of virtual reality or old-school TV, when TV was basically just radio with a screen.

Dad choked on his drink.

"A sonogram." My mother put a name to my brilliant description. "And when have you ever seen footage of the moon landing?"

"Ghost showed me." Well, really Ghost asked Patty to pull it up on her phone because he was trying to convince us that it never happened. He heard these dudes at the bus stop saying it was all fake. Patty said she got a friend whose dad is a rocket scientist (I ain't even know that was a real job!) and that she could prove the moon landing was real. And Sunny, well, he said he already *knew* it was real—the moon landing (and the moon*walk*)—because he had been up there. To the moon. That's what he said. Too bad his discus ain't never go to the moon. Sunny couldn't get that thing to go far enough to land any place other than last place. A few weeks ago, at the first meet he ever threw at, he stepped over the line on the first two tries. Me, Patty, and Ghost started cheering for him. Like, just trying to make sure he ain't feel bad because he was looking pretty rough out there. Even his pops joined in with the encouragement. And then everybody started clapping and screaming *Go Sunny*, and *Come on, Sunny*, and *You can do it*, and all that kind of stuff. Even some people from the other teams. Sunny dropped back in his throwing position and started winding up. His face looked more intense than I'd ever seen it. Like a stone. He wound and wound and wound, then whipped into a spin, and right when he flung the discus, he let out a sound like . . . I don't even know. Like a . . . wail. Like a whale. It was wild. And the discus went maybe . . . ten feet? Maybe. I mean, the thing went nowhere. But he got it off without a foul. And was cheesing from ear to ear. We all were. He threw his hands up in the air, broke out in some kind of weird dance move and everything. Last place. But there were only three people competing, so good thing for him, last place was still . . . third place.

"So, yeah. They gon' sonogram the baby?" I went on.

"Yep, to make sure everything is beating and growing." My mother wiggled her fingers in the air, and even though I couldn't see her feet, I knew she was wiggling her toes, too.

"And you gon' find out if it's a boy?"

"Or . . . a girl," she corrected me.

"Right. Or a girl."

Mom looked at Dad. Then back at me. Nodded, smiling. That was a yes.

"Well, then I'm going to practice."

"Why?" My mother looked shocked, like I said *I* was going to the moon or something.

"So that y'all can come home and surprise me!"

I love surprises. Always have. My folks used to give me surprise birthday parties every year when I was younger, and even though I was never really surprised—because they did it every year—I was still happy they did it, until I asked them to just start surprising me with sneakers for my birthday, so then *I* could surprise the world. My father be surprising my mom all the time with flowers and husband-wife stuff, and my mother surprises us with stuff like turkey wings. I mean, for real for real, this pregnancy was a surprise. Maybe the biggest one ever! Like *BOOM! LU, YOU HAVING A LITTLE BROTHER! Or . . . sister. SURPRISE!*

"O . . . kay." My father caught eyes with my mother, and again, like they rehearsed it, they both shrugged. "Well, obviously neither of us will be able to get you from practice, and we figured you'd want to be there, so we've already made arrangements for, um"—he cleared his throat—"for Coach to bring you home."

I nodded, nibbling on the knobby end of the turkey bone.

"But it's exciting news, right?" My mother's smile

looked like it could split the whole bottom half of her face.

"Yeah." I wiped grease from my mouth with the back of my hand. "But . . . it's a little . . . I don't know. It's . . . I just thought—"

"I know." My dad cut me off, put his fingertips on top of my mother's fingertips. "We did too."

What I was about to say was that I thought Mom couldn't have no more kids. That's what she always said. That's what they always said. That's what they said the doctors always said. According to them, I was a miracle. I wasn't supposed to even be born. So another baby was almost impossible. A miracle with some extra miracle-ness sprinkled on it.

Magic.

Lightning.

Striking. Twice.

2

A NEW NAME FOR PRACTICE: Trying Not to
Play Yourself in Front of a Buncha People

I was born in April. That's the month it rains a lot, so
it make sense that I would be lightning. But this new
baby supposed to be born in December. Ain't no rain
in December. Just snow. So maybe this baby gonna be
more of a snowflake than a lightning bolt. Don't get
me wrong, ain't nothing wrong with snowflakes. They
all different too, except when you got a whole bunch
of them together, then they not snowflakes no more.
They just snow. The only other thing is they don't
really do nothing. Snowflakes just fall on things and
that's it. They just float down and land right on your

nose. Sit there for a second. Then vanish. They beautiful, but not really that big of a deal. Not like lightning.

Lightning don't fall. It strikes. It flashes. Cracks
things. It's hot. Sets things on fire. That's me. I don't
know who future-new-little-baby's about to be, but that's
me. Me and . . . maybe . . . *maybe* this girl named Shante
Morris. She was born in April too—I know because her
mother used to bring nasty cupcakes to school back in
the day—and she definitely might be a lightning kid.
She flash, and cracks, and sets stuff on fire just like me.
Especially people's feelings. Only thing is, Shante don't
look like lightning. She *looks* like a horsefly. And when
you look like a horsefly, people might say you look like
a horsefly. Especially if that "people" is Patty.

We were sitting on the bench at the track, flipping
through the Barnaby Middle School yearbook.

"Yo, I swear Shante Morris still look just like . . . a
horsefly," Patty joked. It was Monday, and almost time
for practice, after the last day of school, which I spent
doing nothing but watching movies and checking
and double-checking my last-day-of-school outfit. No
slipping. Patty told me that she spent *her* last day, or
at least her lunch period, freestyling. Like . . . rapping.
As in, spittin' *bars*. Lyrics. Rhymes. Patty. Talking about
how the rich white girls at her school ain't that great

11

at keeping the beat, but they got good ad-libs and make funny faces, which, when you rapping, is super important. And then that turned into talk about funny faces *outside* of rapping. And that's how Shante Morris and her fly-face came up.

The messed-up part is, Patty knew Shante couldn't help the fact that she had big eyes. *Huge* eyes. Eyes the size of ears. Shante looked like that ever since we were little. Her eyes kinda made her look like she was always surprised at how nasty those cupcakes were every year. Ha! Sorry. But that was . . . Anyway, the only reason Patty was going in on her was because Shante wasn't around to roast Patty to death. Cook her to well-doneness. Spark her up like only lightning can. Shante had so many jokes that we would all gather around in a circle at Barnaby Elementary and just chant "Shut 'em down, Shante, shut 'em down! Shut 'em down, Shante, shut 'em down!" while she barbecued someone who thought it was funny to crack jokes about her big ol' eyes. One of those former victims was the one and only Patina Jones.

"Yo, she don't even have a forehead. Just eyes. She got a eye-head, and when she blink, she can't help but nod, too." Patty blinked her eyes and bowed her head to demonstrate.

"Yeah, okay. Talk all that if you want. But you only saying it because she ain't here to defend herself," I said, and all Patty did was stretch her eyes wide like she was trying to force them to jump out of her face, and continued flipping the pages.

"And look at my girl Cotton. *Ayyyye.* Now, *she* look cute, don't she, Lu?" She held the book up for me to see Cotton's picture, like I ain't have to see her every day at school. It wasn't the gloss on the pages that made it look shiny like that. It was all the Vaseline Cotton always be smearing on because she scared of being ashy and getting unexpectedly fried. By Shante.

"Whatever, Patty." Patty was only teasing me about Cotton because she think I like her and we should go together. But I don't. I do. But not like that. Not all the way. But she cool. But go together? Greasy face? Nah.

"What?" Patty nudged me. "Yes, she do!"

Ghost was walking across the parking lot toward us. Sunny was sitting on the other side of Patty, craning his neck to see the book, all the little rectangle photos of faces and braces, fades and braids, laid out on each page. He never seen a yearbook before, because they don't do yearbooks in homeschool.

"So, wait . . . y'all get these *every* year?" Sunny asked now.

"Every single year. And usually people pass them around to have friends sign them and all that, but I didn't do that just because I already know what every-body gon' say," I explained, grabbing the gold chains around my neck. "Have a good summer, Lu, you *fine-o albino*."

"Boy, shut up." Patty shook her head.

"Yeah, shut up," Ghost repeated, finally reaching us. He dropped his gym bag. "I don't know why Patty said it, but I'm sure you deserve it."

"We just talking about the yearbook. Sunny never seen one before," I said to Ghost, slapping his hand.

"You ain't never seen a yearbook?" Ghost asked. Then he thought about it, kissed his teeth. "Of course, you never seen no yearbook."

"Yo, you should just get that lady who be teaching you—" I started.

"Aurelia," Sunny made clear.

"Yeah, her." I leaned over so I could see Sunny. "Get her to help you make one with pictures of all the stuff y'all did this year. Dance routines and all that."

"You can even do like, Best Dressed, and Most Likely to Succeed, and stuff like that, too. It's just gonna be one student picture in there, but still, might be pretty cool," Ghost added.

"Hmm. I'd get Best Dancer . . . for sure." Sunny nodded, then repeated, "For . . . sure. Seashore. See? Sure . . ."

"Wait, wait." Patty put her hand up, cutting off what was becoming an awkward conversation, which for us, is a normal conversation. "Know what we haven't seen yet?" Her eyes lit up. "The *fine-o albino*'s picture!" With a smirky smile, she immediately started frantically flipping the pages, searching for the *R*s. Searching for me.

"*Chill, chill.* You don't need to see it." I knew it was bad. It was always bad. In pictures I always looked like all flash, no photo. Like floating gold chains.

"Oh, yes we *do*," Ghost chimed in.

"No. You *don't*." I snatched the book from Patty. Stood up so she couldn't snatch it back. "Plus, since we all here, I got something to tell y'all anyway."

"I know what it is, that you—" Patty started to go in, probably about Cotton, but I stopped her.

"Come on, come on. I'm serious." I cut Patty's joke short. Ghost had taken a seat, had slipped off his sliced-up high-tops and was putting on his track shoes. His silver bullets. Sunny was staring at what was left of this week's fading green star. He had one of us draw one on his forearm every meet for good luck. And I

stood in front of them, ready to make my announcement.

"Wassup?" From Ghost.

"Well, last night, I was at home eating turkey
wings—"

"Turkey wings?"

"Patty—"

"Sorry, sorry," she said. "Go 'head."

"So, I'm eating Sunday dinner with my folks, and
then out of nowhere my mother tells me she preg-
nant."

"With what?" Sunny asked, dead serious. Me,
Ghost, and Patty looked at him like he wasn't dead serious with dead-serious faces, even though we knew he
was. Dead. Serious. "Oh . . . you mean, with a human.
Got it."

"But not just any human. My little brother or sister."

"But . . . I thought . . ." Patty's whole face drew up
like it was stuck in a vacuum cleaner hose.

"Exactly! That's why it's such a big deal."

"Wow." That's what Ghost said. Then he got more
excited. "Dude . . . wow! You gon' be somebody big
bro!"

"Oh boy," Patty huffed, but I knew she was joking. "Well, at least now you can stop pretending to be

mine. Congrats, dummy." She jumped up, threw an arm around me, yoked my neck.

"Yeah, dude, that's big. Congrats . . . for real," Ghost followed. "You happy?"

Happy. Hmm. I had been asking myself that all night, all day. Thought about it this morning when I said my mantra—*I'm the man, the kid, the guy.* Thought about it when I was rubbing sunscreen into my lightning skin, rubbing and rubbing and rubbing and rubbing. When I put my chains around my neck, my earrings in, my clothes on. *Pose. Pose. Kill 'em. Smooth.* And I was still thinking about it. Happy.

"Yeah," I kinda squeaked. "I mean, of course it's gonna be weird having a little kid around all of a sudden, but . . . yeah. I think I'm happy." Patty cocked her head. "I'm happy." I did a closed-mouth smile that was supposed to say, *stop asking me questions*, but judging by the way Ghost looked at me all squinty-eyed, I knew he knew it was something else. Luckily, before *he* could *say* something else, Sunny barged in.

"Let's toast!"

"Toast?" You never know with Sunny. He might've pulled out four pieces of bread he was saving for a special occasion. Or in his head, he might be a grown-up and be really talking about a toast with the glass-clinking and all that. But then he reached down and dug his hands in the dirt and grass, snatched a clump.

"Do it," he said in a un-Sunny-like, way-too-serious tone. So we all did it. Just held fists full of dirt and grass. "Now, together." Sunny held his fist out, and Patty put hers to his, then Ghost put his to theirs, and I completed the cheesy fist bump—a four-fist clover—by adding mine to the mix. "Lu, we love you, and . . . ," Sunny started, but got a little choked up. Now *that* was *very* Sunny. "And we wanna congratulate you on your baby human sibling." Then he yelled out, "Boomticky tacky cheers!" and opened his hand and let the dirt and grass fall back to the ground. And so we all opened our hands and did the same. And I won't lie, it was actually kind of cool. Until . . .

"Newbies! What y'all doing? It's the last week of practice and *now* y'all decide to play in the dirt? How about we play on the track? What y'all think about that?" Coach barked, right on time, as usual. Right on time, means right on the wrong time, which is no time for fun time.

I slapped my hands together, brushing dust from my palms, and headed over to the track, where the rest of the team was. Mikey and Brit-Brat and Deja and Krystal and Freddy and J.J. and Curron and Lynn, and Melissa, and . . . Chris. *Chris?* What was he doing here?

Chris Myers. He was a long-leg. Ran the eight hundred. And good at it too. He started off on the team but quit after the first meet. Just all of a sudden, gone. But now he was back, which was weird because it was the *end* of the season.

"Thanks for joining us, *assistant* captain." Yep, Aaron was there too. Being a jerk. Of course. He started bumping his gums as soon as I set foot on the track. Mad that I worked my way up to co-captain as a newbie. Scared I was going to outshine him, which wouldn't have been hard to do. Aaron was fast but not fast enough. I, on the other hand, was the fastest runner on the whole team besides Ghost, and we were basically the same. Traded first place every meet. Plus, I was *definitely* the flyest.

"*Co*-captain," I corrected him. "Ain't nobody your assistant." I eyed Aaron from heel to head.

"Yeah, whatever," Aaron replied under his breath. "Ain't nobody my assistant . . . but you."

"Okay, okay," Coach started in, stopping me from saying anything else. "Let's talk. First thing first. Let's welcome Chris back to the squad. Though he normally runs the eight hundred, he's agreed to step up and run Sunny's mile, since Sunny obviously won't be." Lynn sucked her teeth so loud that it sounded like a single clap. Coach eyeballed her but let it slide. "We need him. We need every single one of you at your best. This is the last week of the season. The *last*. And I know y'all want me to tell you all the good things you've done. I know you want me to praise you, and, honestly, y'all deserve some praise. But I don't have time for that. *We* don't have time for it. We're four practices away from this year's championship meet. And you know what I always say—"

We all knew where this was going, so we joined in and finished it for him.

"The best never rest." There was just enough punch on it for Coach to not be mad, but we definitely dragged it out in that this-is-so-annoying way. All of us. Even Chris. Even Aaron.

"Exactly. The best . . . never . . . rest. And we are the best. And all that means is more work. We have to see it all the way through to the end. Got me?"

Everybody nodded, and a few people—mainly Aaron—chirped like a suck-uppy bird, "Got you, Coach."

"Good." Coach nodded. "At least the weather's

on our side. Not too hot. Nice breeze out here. So let's stretch it out. After you knock out your warm-ups, Lu, you come talk to me."

After the stretches and the lazy laps—Aaron always led the laps, and because of that they were always way too slow—I went through to the fence where Coach and Whit were going over the game plan for the last week of the season. Whit blew her whistle and got everybody else ready to do what we always did on Mondays—fart licks. Basically, you just run kinda fast for like two or three minutes, then run *real* fast for one. Over and over and over again. Brutal.

"How's the ankle?" Coach asked, staring down at it. He asked because after our last track meet, I had a slight limp. See, I usually run the hundred meter and the two hundred meter, and even though I don't run the four hundred meter, if I did, I'd smoke it. It'd be Aaron's first second-place ribbon of the year. Because I'm a *true* sprinter. Everybody and their mama know how I get down. Been sprinting since, well . . . a long time. But for the last month I've been training for a new event. An extra one. The 110-meter hurdles. And I ain't gon' front, I . . . I just . . .

Here's the thing. When you look at a hurdle, it don't really seem like that big of a deal until you get right up on it. You gotta time it just right, and pump your heart big enough to get your leg up and over the bar. You can't just hop it like you hop over everything else, like a fire hydrant or a park bench. You gotta literally gallop over it like some kind of horse. But I ain't no horse. I'm a human. A not-so-tall human.

At the last meet—my first time finally running hurdles—when I came up on that first one, even though I'd been practicing, I just got nervous and second-guessed it and my timing got thrown off and my heart got small. So even though I got over it, I clipped the second hurdle and went down. Like a clown. Hard. And my ankle did something funny. Something not funny. Something hurting. It ain't broke or nothing like that. Just bruised. And sore. But not as sore as the part of me that likes to win and hates to be played out in front of a buncha people. The funny, not-so-funny thing was, ain't nobody laugh. Nobody. Not even Aaron's corny, butt-kissing mouth. Everybody just *oooooh*'d, which is almost worse than *haaaaaaa*. Because *oooooh* is like pity. So, it sucked.

"It's fine," I said. And I know when people say stuff like, *Really Coach, I'm fine. I swear*, they don't be fine. But I was.

"Okay. Next question: Do you want to work on

hurdles today or not? If you don't, that means you won't run it Saturday." I opened my mouth to say something, but Coach put his hand to my chest, cut me off. "And that's okay. We can focus on it next season. Plus, if everybody wins their races, including Chris, and Sunny places at least second in discus, we'll take the championship." Coach shrugged as if he didn't just ask me the trickiest trick question of all time. He just heard us all say *the best never rest* a few minutes before, and now he was basically asking me if I wanted to quit. And I knew he didn't mean quit running, or even quit hurdling, he just meant maybe taking a pause. But to me, especially when it comes to this sport, pausing and quitting is the same thing.

"No. I wanna work on it. I can do it," I replied.

Coach nodded, but he looked at me like he ain't believe me. He do that all the time, with all of us. It usually comes right before he spits some extra spaced-out, what-is-Coach-talkin'-'bout talk at us. But this time, he just said, "Okay. Let's get to it."

And Fart Lick Monday became Make It Over Monday. Or more like, Get Over Not Getting Over It Monday, for me.

3

A NEW NAME FOR RIDING IN A CAB:
Trapped in a Rolling Room with Roommates Who Think They Know Everything in the Whole World

Can't nothing really prepare you for the moment your coach, a man who don't even really have eyebrows on his face, gets down on all fours in the middle of the track and yells for you to come jump over him. Nothing. But that's what was happening. And . . . yeah.

"Let's see it," Coach called out.

"Um. See . . . what?" I was standing at the starting line. At first I thought Coach was trying to be funny. Cracking a joke, to see how far I'd go with it.

"Your hurdle." Coach flung his hand out like he

was waving me toward him. His back had a hump in it, arched and uncomfortable-looking. "Come hurdle me." Honestly, this was one of the strangest things I've ever heard Coach say, and he says a lot of strange things. He was always doing stuff like this, but this was on another level. It just seemed . . . wrong.

"Just . . . jump?"

He nodded.

"Over you?"

He nodded again. Then backtracked and said, "Well, no. Don't *jump*, Lu." *Phew, thank goodness.* Then Coach added, "*Hurdle* me. Low speed. Now let's go. On my whistle."

Wha?

I made sure my chains were tucked into my fitted jersey to keep them from slapping me in the face, then got in position. Coach put the whistle in his mouth.

Badeep!

I took off, running only a little faster than a jog, and as I approached Coach I just . . . jumped—like, hopped—over him, before hitting the brakes. The whole thing was stupid. It was like a bunny hop. A leapfrog.

"I told you *not* to jump," Coach reminded me, and I was immediately happy everybody else was busy "fart licking," and that my mother wasn't still doing the whole sit-in-the-stands-and-watch-her-boy-practice-every-day thing, like at the beginning of the season.

"I know, but you so low to the ground it just don't make sense to—"

"It doesn't matter that I'm a smaller hurdle. We approach it the same. Small, big, whatever. So, this time I want you to hurdle me. *Her—dull—me.* Lead with the knee." Coach, still on the ground, put the whistle back in his mouth, then took it out just to add, "Now get on your mark." Whistle back between teeth.

Badeep!

I took off again, this time a little faster, hurdling Coach like he asked—knee first—jumping way, way over him.

"Better! But you're running like you're running a regular dash. So you're keeping your body low for too long. But that's not what this is. Gotta get up quicker." Coach sat up, rested on his knees, and started pumping his arms to demonstrate what I was supposed to look like, even though if I looked like he looked, then I'd look like ridiculous. Like a turtle trying to speed up. "Got me? Let's go."

Badeep!

"Better. Again."

Badeep!

"Don't get lazy. Again."

I felt so silly, but I kept doing it. Kept running, faster and faster toward Coach, leaping over him—way over him, over and over again. Until, finally, he stood up.

"How's the ankle?" he asked for the second time.

"It's . . . cool." I tried to catch my breath.

"You sure?"

"Yeah, yeah . . . I'm good."

And I guess Coach took that as, I'm ready for something tougher. A real hurdle. Because he went and grabbed one that was off to the side of the track and dragged it over into the fourth lane, where he had just been acting like a human hurdle. "Back on the line."

Coach stood to the side, blew the whistle, and I started sprinting down the track again. And right when I got to the hurdle . . . I pulled up. I just couldn't jump it. I felt like maybe my rhythm was off or something. Like I was going to clip it like I did at the meet.

"What happened?" Coach asked.

"Nothing," I answered. "Let's do it again."

I went back to the starting line, and this time ain't even wait for the whistle. Just took off. *Lead with the* knee. *Hurdle it.* But as soon as I got a few steps away, one second from the metal legs and wooden bar, it got taller. At least in my mind it did. So I dipped off to the side and went around it.

I don't know how to explain this, but I was so . . . I just felt . . . stupid. I should've been able to do this. I'd been training to do it for almost a month, and was doing pretty good jumping them until the last meet, my first time really running the actual race. And then the crash. I should've been able to jump this thing because . . . I could. I can do anything. At least on the track. Shoot, I would even run the mile if Coach ain't bring Chris back. I don't know how good I would've done, but I think I could've at least done okay. After all, I'm the man. The kid. The guy. Lucky. Lookie. Lucky-Nobody-on-the-Team-Was-Looking, Lu.

I started back down the track when Coach called out to me.

"That's enough for today." That's what he said, but what I heard was, *You can't do it.* Felt like I got punched in the back.

"No, no. Coach, just let me try one more—"

"Fall in with Ghost and give me some fartleks for the rest of practice. We'll try something else tomorrow."

I ain't argue. I wanted to, but nah.

➤

After practice me and Ghost helped Coach put cones and discuses and whatever other track things he'd pulled from his cab's treasure trunk back in it. Most of the team had already left except Krystal and Brit-Brat, who were putting in some extra drills with Whit, who was timing them. Patty and Sunny had already bounced.

"Lu, I'm just gon' let you know right now, don't be trying to ride in my limo all the time. I know it's a piece of junk, but it's *my* piece of junk," Ghost joked, sliding into the backseat. I slid in beside him, slammed the door.

"Oh, *really*?" Coach said from up front, yanking his seat belt across his chest. "If I'm your chauffeur, you owe me some cash, *Castle*." He dragged Ghost's name and rubbed the tips of his thumb and index finger together. "*A lot* of it."

"Man, what you askin' me for? Lu got all the money. You see how he be out here flashing on us. The gold chain god. Glass in his ears—"

"These *diamonds*, boy." I had to let him know.

"Exactly. You heard him, Coach. *Diamonds*." Ghost slapped me on the arm. "Pay the man!"

"Yeah, whatever."

As we pulled out of the parking lot and started toward Glass Manor—we were dropping Ghost off first, since he didn't live that far from the park—Ghost started running through ideas for names for my future little brother or sister.

"I'm thinking Ghost, if it's a boy. And if it's a girl . . . Ghost," he suggested.

"No."

"Why not? Ghost is such a good name for a boy or girl. Like Alex. Or Aaron."

"Aaron?" Coach said. He was on the phone talking to his wife, Mrs. Margo. They were talking about their baby son, Tyrone, and how the weather was irritating him. Allergies. Ghost was irritating me—allergies—and now Coach was chiming in.

"Yeah, you never knew a girl named Aaron?"

"Hold on, honey," he said into the ridiculous can-I-take-your-order headset he was wearing. Then shot back at Ghost, "No. I've met young ladies named Erin, though."

"That's what I said, Aaron."

"Right, and I said *Erin*. Not Aaron. *Erin*."

"What the? Coach . . . you saying the same thing. Aaron."

"No—"

"Don't matter, y'all. Aaron or . . . whatever different version of that name Coach keep saying, *definitely* ain't happening." I shut that down.

"Okay, what about Castle?"

"What about *shut up*?"

"Hmmm." Ghost did a *so-so* hand wag. "I just think Li'l Shut Up would have a tough life." He shook his head. Coach laughed and whispered something—I know, about us—to his wife.

Driving through Glass Manor wasn't much different from driving through Barnaby Terrace, except folks around Glass Manor lived in buildings, and we lived in connected houses. Row homes. We lived side by side. They lived up and down. Either way, we all sharing walls. Plus the vibe is the same. People on the block talking, kids tossing a football back and forth across the street, heaving it at just the right height. High enough to get it over oncoming cars, but low enough to not clip the telephone wires. Music from somebody inside. Music from everybody outside.

When we pulled up to Ghost's apartment, he opened the car door, and as soon as he got a leg out, Coach started up.

"Hold up. Wait one second," he said, flipping his hand behind him, palm up. "Ten smackers, please."

Ghost smacked Coach's hand and said, "How 'bout a five," then jumped out of the car and slammed the door. Coach rolled the window down and yelled, "I quit! Better lace them fancy silver sneakers up and get ready to walk home from now on!" Ghost ignored him. Then Coach looked at me through the rearview. "Wanna get up front?"

"Nah, I'm good back here," I said, leaning against the door.

"Get up front." Coach's voice thickened. So I got up front.

As we pulled away from Glass Manor, away from Ghost's apartment and the noise of up-and-down life, Coach asked, "So, tell me, you scared to jump hurdles now?"

"Scared to jump 'em?" I repeated, looking at the side of Coach's face. Ghost always said he looked a little like a turtle, and he was right. But a mad turtle. Almost like a Ninja Turtle. Coach scratched his chest, his T-shirt tugging down, showing the dark tattoo around his neck. "Um . . . not really," I said. "But I am scared of *not* jumping 'em and breaking my whole body up. You saw what happened on Saturday. I ain't built for that kind of embarrassment, Coach. Plus I'm way too pretty for bruises." I thought that was funny—a joke—but

Coach didn't laugh or crack a smile or nothing. Just stopped the car. We hadn't even made it all the way off Ghost's block yet. He just whipped the cab over next to a parked truck and slapped his blinkers on.

"I'm just jokin'. *Dang.*" I tried to explain, but Coach tightened his face, bit down on his bottom lip like a lemon eater.

He turned away from me, looked out the window, letting the words sit between us for a second. I thought about changing the subject and telling him about new-future-little-baby, but instead I just ain't say nothing. Already said enough. Just leaned over to see who Coach was looking at, now waving at. An old man, maybe fifty. Maybe sixty. Hard to tell because his face looked forty but his body looked eighty. He was sweeping the sidewalk. Walking beside him was another dude, a guy with an old body *and* an old face, but he had a wild jumpy bop. And it was obvious he was buzzing and bothering the young-faced old man about something.

Coach rolled the window down.

"Everything all right, Mr. Jeff?" Coach asked. Youngface turned toward the cab.

"Hey now, Otis." He lifted the broom in the air like a magic wand. "I'm fine. I'm fine. But . . . I'm tired of trying to convince this fool to get away from me before I sweep him up with the rest of the mess the wind done blown around out here. I got a daughter just like him, always beggin' beggin' beggin'. I'm taking care of her son right now while she tries to get herself together, so *all* my money—every red cent—is going to the Goodwill and his belly. Grandson gon' eat me out of a house, a home, and into a doggone hole." The old man shook his head, hard. "And now this joker here come talking about sparing some change. He got some nerve."

Coach lifted his butt off the seat, just high enough to slide his wallet from his back pocket. He slipped a dollar from the fold.

"Here." Coach held the single out the window, not for the man called Mr. Jeff, but for the jumpy man (Oldface) behind him, who came shuffling across the street. He walked like all the bones in his body were broken. Like his legs were only being held together by string. A puppet with an invisible puppet master.

"Hey, hey . . . Otis, man, I appreciate this. You know I'm hard up right now. You know . . . I mean, I . . . I . . . I just need to get something to eat. You know how it is. Just something to eat. That's all," the man jittered, the sound of his words like wheezes, like he couldn't speak and breathe at the same time. He smelled like burning things. Sweat. And rotten.

Coach just nodded. Swallowed. Rolled the window up. Then finally turned back to me.

"You wanna talk about *embarrassment*?" Coach chewed on the sentence, crunched it like Ghost does sunflower-seed shells. "Tomorrow, why don't you ask Whit about it?"

"Whit?"

Coach nodded and changed the subject. "Let me ask you something, pretty boy. Your daddy ever mention the name Torrie Cunningham to you?"

Did he ever. Torrie Cunningham was like a legend in Barnaby Terrace. My father talked about this dude all the time. Said nobody around here really watched track back in the day until Torrie started running for Barnaby High. Everybody called him the Wolf, because when he would pass you, instead of the *woop woop* sound everybody in the crowd makes, Torrie would just howl. Like, he would be on your heels howling at your back, and then the whole crowd would howl as he zoomed past. I had to listen to those stories all the time. Dad said the three years Torrie ran were the only three years track was more popular than basketball. But he never made it big because he quit running his senior year. So, yeah. I knew all about him. So I told Coach, "My dad always be talking about him."

"Well, I ran against him." Coach shook his head. "The Wolf was noooo joke. Ran like his parents were breeze and wind. Like he was born to do that, and just that." Coach grinned, and then he didn't. "The Wolf could've been the G.O.A.T. Know where he is now?"

I figured the Wolf was probably coaching a high school team or something like that. Either that or coaching another young elite team for us to dust on Saturday, and maybe that's why Coach was bringing him up.

"Where?" I asked.

"Right there." Coach knocked a knuckle on the window. Then yanked the stick thing, put the car back in drive, and pulled out.

"Wait, that guy is—" I tried to get another glimpse of the old-faced man through the back window but couldn't.

"The Wolf." Coach nodded. "His senior year he got caught up in what a lot of us got caught up in. What my old man got caught up in. See, Torrie was howling and all that, but he was never a wolf. And we all realized that when he met a *real* one and got eaten alive, from the inside out. These days, if he ain't over here bothering Mr. Jeff, he over at the basketball court jumping around, out of his head, but . . . I don't know. To me, *that's* embarrassment. Not the dope—*that's* illness. But to let something get in the way of your full potential . . ." Coach glanced in the rearview, adjusted it slightly, then looked back at the road. "Actually, maybe I can't say that. Because the thing that's beating him, he never stood a chance against. He's not jumping over a hurdle, son. That brother back there's jumping over a mountain." Whoa. Guess I *didn't* know everything about Torrie Cunningham.

"Yeah. Okay," I said. "But . . . what that gotta do with Whit?" I was trying to understand what the heck Coach was talking about. He was always all over the place. A grown-up Sunny.

"Oh. Right." Coach turned the wheel to the left and the car floated in that direction. "He's her big brother. That's why me and Whit work together so well. Why we connect. We've seen what's out here for talented kids, like you. The wonders . . . and, unfortunately, the wolves."

I stayed quiet again, Coach's words pricking me like I was sitting in the middle of a giant hairbrush. That dude, the one back there begging and moving like he was trying on a new body for the first time, was Whit's big brother, one of the best runners in Glass Manor (and every other neighborhood around here) history? That dude? Really? That was enough to make me itch. Enough to make me try to scratch my head down to the brain. See if I could get it to understand.

The Wolf. That guy was the Wolf. Wolves howl. Growl. Flash their teeth. Wolves bite. I bit the dust. Jumping hurdles. Jumping Coach. Coach and Whit. Whit and Wolf. Wolf a big bro. I'm almost a big bro. Will be in December. Snowflakes in December. Snow is white. I'm white. But not really. Not really. Really the man. The kid. The guy. Focus. That was the Wolf. The Wolf. Maybe I'm what he would've been if he wasn't bit. But I'm . . .

"Here we are. The Palace of Lu," Coach announced, finally pulling up in front of my house. The tone of his voice had some joke in it again, but I could tell it was still attached to some serious.

"Good-lookin' on the ride," I said, not scratching no more, but still kinda . . . surprised. But not in the good way. I held my fist out for a pound.

"This one's on me," Coach joked. "And, uh, you can thank me tomorrow by cutting out all that *embarrassment* nonsense. Sometimes we fall. It happens. Plus, I don't even know what you so worked up about anyway. Especially today. I was the one being a human hurdle. And I didn't care *what* I looked like. You know why? Because sometimes I gotta be who I am for you to know it's okay for you to be who you are." He knocked his fist against mine.

"Well, that's you, Coach. But I ain't no human hurdle," I explained. "Plus, I already know who I am." I rubbed my chin like my dad does when he smooths out his beard. *The man. The kid.*

"So do I." Coach smirked, yanking the car back in drive. "Embarrassed."

I looked at him, put my thoughts on mute for a moment. "Come on, Coach. I was *joking.* You don't know what a joke is? For real for real . . . I wasn't really embarrassed. I mean, I was, but really I was just—"

"Oh, *I* know, *I* know. I got it," he cut me off, now full-on smiling. "Scared."

4

A NEW NAME FOR LITTLE BROTHER:
Little Sister

Gordon. That's my dad's real name. But everybody calls him Goose. Everybody. Except my mom. And me. I call him Dad. Actually, I called his phone when I got in the house and found out he and my mother weren't there yet. So tonight, I called him . . . *Late* Dad.

"*Late* Dad? That's the best you got, Lu?" he joked me about my bad joke. Which made it a worse joke. I could hear him turn away from the phone and tell my mother that I called him Late Dad, and then I could hear my mother say, "Late Dad? Wow. *Nice one*, son. Really clever." She sounded disappointed, but a funny kind of disappointed. Honestly, I couldn't blame her. The joke was trash. But come on, I can't be great at *everything*. Plus he's my father so it ain't like I could just say, *Where you at, you booboo-faced clown?* I mean, I could have, but why run the risk of future-new-little-baby ending up an only child?

Anyway, ten minutes after that goofy phone call, my mom and dad got home. I was just about to get in the shower and wash the track funk off me before dinner, but doubled back to get the big baby surprise that I wanted but didn't really want. But did. But didn't. But kinda needed to want. Or was supposed to want. And did. But . . . didn't.

"Nope. Absolutely not!" Dad pointed back down the hall toward the bathroom. "We ain't telling you nothing, because it's impossible to talk and hold our breath at the same time, *Stinky Son.*"

"Yeah, *Stinky Son,*" my mom joined in just to be funny. She was his all-the-time hype-man. Hype-woman. "You smell like . . . old bananas!"

"And you smell like mom jokes," I tossed back at her, swiping under my arms, then sniffing. I knew I stank, but for some reason I just needed to make sure.

"Then I smell like *YOU!*" she shouted, her voice cracking into a big laugh. "Only difference is, I'm actually a mom. A mother of . . . two." She put two fingers in the air. "And you, banana boy, won't know if the other is a sister or brother until you smell less like your daddy after a long day."

"Wow." From me.

Dad snapped his neck toward her. "I thought we were on the same team!"

"I know." Shrug. "We are."

"Wow." From me, again.

"So then why you gotta bring me into this! I don't stink!" he whined, sounding like he felt played out.

"No, honey," my mother replied, lifting her voice to cartoon tone. She kissed my dad, then thumbed her nose. "You . . . um . . . you don't stink . . . at all."

I took a long shower. The washing part happened quick, but I just stood there in the water, thinking about future-new-little-baby and how weird it was going to be hearing all that crying, and smelling the poop, and holding something smaller than a watermelon. I always wanted to have a little brother. Somebody I could look at and it would be like looking at me through a brown filter. Probably a less cool brown filter, but still a brown filter, because the chance of Mom having another albino baby was almost impossible. But now that it was happening—like really happening—it felt funny.

Because, honestly, I was kind of like a miracle (that's what they say), but if there's *another* miracle, then the first one just becomes a cool thing that happened. But not . . . a miracle no more. And even though being different is tough, being different is different.

But still, it'll be cool. It'll be cool. It'll be cool, yeah. Of course it will. Definitely. Plus, no matter what, it won't be as hard to be a big brother as it is to jump hurdles. And I ain't scared of that, so ain't no way I was gonna be scared of this. No matter what Coach was talking about.

After the longest shower of all time, I threw on some sweats and headed back to the kitchen, the smell of leftover turkey meat floating through the air.

I sat down. Elbows on the table. Deep breath. "Okay. I'm ready."

"For what?" my mother asked, nudging my arms off and taking a seat. My father was washing his hands in the sink.

"Um . . . for the surprise."

I felt something hit the back of my head. A balled-up paper towel.

"Surprise!" Dad yelped.

"Ha. Ha. Ha," I fake-laughed, slapping my father on the back as he sat next to me.

He tucked his chains, then picked up his turkey wing and bit straight into it, caveman-style. Chewed and chewed, while I stared at him, waiting and waiting. Then I looked at my mother. She turned away.

"Mom!"

"Okay, okay." She broke. "You're gonna be a big brother."

I cocked my head, annoyed. *"Seriously."*

Both of my parents busted out laughing, turkey-meat confetti flying from my dad's mouth. Gross.

"Okay, okay. Here we go, for real this time." Mom took a deep breath. "We have ourselves . . . ," she revved up.

A boy.

"A . . ."

Snowflake. But a snowflake boy. Just say it.

"Boy!" she yelped.

"I knew it!"

"Named Lu."

"Wait . . . *what?*"

"But what we're *about* to have is . . . a girl!" My mother shrieked and my father threw his greasy hands in the air, clapped them over his head. Mom rubbed her stomach. "You're gonna have a little sister!"

A sister. I felt . . . okay, let me explain. It's not

that I wanted, um . . . that I was kind of hoping for a little brother because I don't like girls. It ain't that at all. I do like girls. Patty been acting like my sister for forever, and, you know, it's cool. But to have a little brother would've been good for me, y'know, like I said before, just because I wanted to see what I would've looked like if I was . . . brown. And me being a boy and all, I just felt like it made sense to look into another boy's face to see my own.

"What's wrong?" my mother asked, which let me know that I wasn't doing a good job at keeping my face happy, and I imagined it probably looked like I was forcing a smile, and when you force a smile, it always looks like you're trying to ignore the fact that your stomach's bubbling.

"Nothing."

"Lu." My dad had finally got the turkey meat down. I looked at him. "Say it."

"It's . . . really, it ain't like a big thing. I'm cool. Happy." I'd been practicing that. "I just wanted . . ."

"A little brother," Mom said. She reached over, grabbed my hand, which I had balled into a fist and was pushing my thumb between the fingers. "Right?"

"I ain't even know you could have more kids, but then you say you having one all of a sudden and so I

45

just wanted to know . . . what I would look like . . . I know he might not have looked just like me, or whatever, but still, it would've at least been cool to know what I would've looked like if I was . . . normal."

"Normal?" Mom's face twitched. "You know how I feel about—"

"I know, I know," I cut her off. "But you know what I mean." She hated when I said things like *normal*. Because when I say normal, I mean brown, and she don't feel like the color of my skin makes me un-normal. But if that's true, then why would she call me a lightning bolt? To be one in seventeen thousand ain't normal, and when seventeen thousand (million) people are just staring at you like you a freak, it sometimes be feeling . . . off.

"I know. But can I tell you something? Your little sister might not look like you—"

"Or she might," my father interrupted, a finger in the air.

"True. She might. But even if she doesn't look *like* you, she *is* going to look *at* you. And you know what she's gonna see?" My mother followed my eyes, making sure she didn't lose me.

"Yep. The most handsome boy to ever go to Barnaby Middle." I forced a joke. And another smile. Then lowered my head.

was back in the day. He was going on and on about him. The Wolf. Mr. . . . what's his name. Torrie—"

"Cunningham. The fastest kid I ever seen." Dad, now all perked up, took his hands out his pockets and rubbed them together, ready to tell me a story I had already heard like a trillion times. The Wolf. The howl. The speed. Again. "He would talk so. Much. Trash. So cocky, but it didn't matter because nobody could beat him."

"But you ain't never tell me that he all messed up now. We saw him today—Coach dropped off Ghost before me—in Glass Manor, buggin' *out*."

My father stopped the hand rubbing mid-rub and sighed. "Yeah, I know." Even though he ain't wash not one dish, he reached over and turned the faucet off.

"I'm not done yet," I said, but Dad ain't care.

"Lu, you know how I got the name Goose?" What is it about grown-up men and changing the subject? It's like moms always ask what's wrong, and dads always say, *let's talk about something else.* Truth is, I never even thought about the Goose thing. No one ever brought it up. I hadn't even brought it up. It just—was. I was talking about Wolf, and here he go, jumping animals.

"I don't think so."

"Well, when I was young, I used to stutter." He

jammed his fingers back in his pockets. "I mean really, really stutter. It was bad. I could barely get a sentence out. And when the words would get stuck in my throat, I would jerk my neck almost like I was trying to cough 'em up. And I did it so much—bobbing my head like a chicken or a goose—that that's what people started calling me." He bobbed his head a few times, then continued. "Well, mainly it was one dude." Now Dad started smiling. Not a full smile. Just a smile of remembrance, which usually be small smiles. A peek of teeth. "Otis."

"Who . . . Oh, you mean . . . *Coach?*"

"Coach. He gave me that name. We were kids growing up together in Glass Manor. My folks used to take care of him whenever his mother was working, and his dad was in and out, struggling with dope. We were like brothers, actually. Even joined the high school track team together. He was great. I was . . . okay. My mother pushed me to run because she knew I'd be with Otis and felt like track was keeping us both out of trouble. And it was, but I wasn't good enough to stop people from teasing me about my stutter. I would run my race and get third place, and to celebrate me—to *cheer* for me—my own teammates would cluck and flap their arms and go, *Guh-Guh-Guh-Guh Goose!*"

"Wait. Coach flamed you? Because that don't really sound like something he would do."

Dad flipped his eyes up in his head. "First of all, we didn't call it 'flaming' back then. And we were young. And I don't think he, or any of them, meant it to be mean. It was just something everybody was in on," Dad said, brushing off the question. "But after a while it started really getting to me. So I quit. I wanted to be a winner, Lu. To be cool. And at the time, I couldn't see nothing down the line in my life. I could only see what was right in front of me. And what was in front of me was stuttering and Goose jokes. So at fifteen I decided to do the only other thing I saw as cool around my way."

"Sell drugs."

"Right. I've told you that before, and you know I'm not proud of it. And you know if you *ever* even think about—"

"I know, and I'm not." I put my hands up quick.

"Anyway"—my dad sucked in a long breath—"to bring this back around to Torrie, there were a lot of people jealous of him. Dude was unbeatable and he felt, and acted, like nothing could get him. Like nothing could happen to him. And people hated it. You should've seen him. He walked around like a celebrity.

Be signing autographs and all that. It was nuts. But he also had so much pressure on him. I mean, he was seventeen and the track was supposed to be his way out. There were coaches and recruiters fighting over him. So just before the championship meet, his junior year, he asked me if I had something that could give him some extra speed. He really wanted to impress the colleges, and by then, everybody knew I had *everything*. Stuff to put people down, stuff to take people up. I had it all. So I met him, served him, and that was that."

"You sold the Wolf his first hit?" I asked, gaping at my dad, just to make sure I was catching it all.

Dad nodded, then dropped another bomb. "Unfortunately, I also ended up selling Otis's dad, Mr. Brody . . . his last."

All the words in my head went away. Shut down. Thoughts, gone. And a few seconds later my mind came back on, like a reboot. But I was still confused about what my father was telling me. I mean, I could hear his words, but none of them were making sense. I mean, they were. But they weren't.

"Wha . . . what? *What?*" I said, my brain still on fuzz. On *loading*. "Do he know that? Do Coach know you—"

"Look, Lu, I work every day, every single day trying

to make it right," Dad said, his face becoming weird, as if he was wearing a mask of his own face . . . on his face. That was my cue to ease up on the questions. "You know that."

I did.

I do.

But still.

My dad's job—the job that had him working so hard that he was never around—was basically being like a rehab hustler. Always out at basketball courts, and on hot corners, and anywhere else he knew there would be people having a tough time with drugs, and the same hand-to-hand he used to do when he was younger, he did in a different way now. Now he slips them tiny ziplock bags with notes in them. Notes he be getting from family members. Their brothers and sisters and kids and cousins. And if, after reading those notes, an addict felt like he might want to try getting clean, my pops would personally take them to the rehab place, help them do all the paperwork stuff, and get them back in touch with their families. Back to themselves.

"The point I'm trying to make with all this is, when I see you, I see the me *before* all that. Before the smoke. The rock and the junk. Before the flash and the fly.

When I look at you, I see the me with potential. The me, who was . . . different, but good"—he pointed to my chest—"in here. I don't care what you lose, kid. Just don't lose that." Dad rubbed my head, yanked me close. "You're gonna be a good big brother, Lu. Hear me?" I heard him, but I ain't say nothing. "Matter fact, and I haven't talked to your mother about this yet but I think she'll be okay with it, I want you to think of a name for your new little sister."

"A nickname?"

"No." My father took his arm from around me. "Her name."

Her real name.

Whoa.

5

A NEW NAME FOR SPRINTING: Surviving Stinky Dudes Who Got Nothing Better to Do Than Talk Trash Because They Haters

Christina. That's my mom's name. And that's what she go by. Christina. Either that or Mom, or Mrs. Richardson, which is what kids call her, unless you Patty or Cotton. Then you call her Mama Richardson, the babysitter. Because that's what she was when we were younger. And by younger, I mean a few years ago, before Patty moved away from Barnaby Terrace to live with her aunt and uncle (and started eating turkey wings like she fancy), and Cotton started staying at home with her older brother, Skunk. But I hate the word "babysitter," because we weren't babies, and we definitely weren't being sat on. We barely even sat down. If anything, we were always up, jumping around while my mom put together these super-hard dance routines with all kinds of ticks and booms to old-head jams with Cotton and Patty. And . . . me. I would try, but I ain't really no dancer, so the girls would always tell me to take a time-out, which was their fake-nice way of telling me I danced like a door, opening and closing, and that I should just pretend to be an audience member at their make-believe concert. *Take a seat, Lu. Several seats.*

"Clap louder!" Cotton would snip at me. And my mom would just go along.

But Mom's babysitting (child look-aftering) life is over—been over—and now she the queen of fruit sculptures. Sculptures . . . made of . . . fruit. Okay, so maybe not sculptures. Sunny been showing me real sculptures of old white people without arms, and even though they look weird, what my mother be making ain't nowhere near as sculpture-y as that. She just makes, like, artsy things with watermelons and cantaloupes, funny-looking faces with grape eyes, and strawberry noses, and slices of the green melon I can never remember the name of, as the smiles. I know it sounds kinda silly, but business is booming. She was even on one of those morning shows—even though I barely recognized her because of all the makeup they put on her. On there showing people how to turn a pineapple into a boat.

That's my mom. A trained artist. Went to art school and everything but put it all on pause after she had me. Now she's back to it and has become the Picasso of Produce.

I ain't make that up. She did.

And she calls me the Orange Master. It's not another nickname. It's more like a title. And because school was out, on Tuesday morning the Orange Master had no choice but to get to work.

"Sleep well?" Mom asked as I came into the kitchen.

"I slept okay," I said, the taste of toothpaste sour on my tongue. Coffee in the air. "You supposed to be drinking coffee with a baby in there?" I asked, grabbing the handle of the fridge.

"It's a half cup. Sheesh."

"If you say so."

"So . . . just okay?" she asked again about my sleep, not letting it go.

"Yeah, just okay." The truth is that I slept pretty good, but it took a while for me to get there. For my brain to stop moving around, thinking about what my father told me. I already knew about his past. About his time in the street and how he'd changed. But I never thought about who he sold to. About who those people's families might've been. Like Coach. Like Whit. Like who knows who else. And then when I finally got those thoughts to chill, new thoughts popped in there, like, *I can't believe I'm having a little sister. A sister. Little girl. And me. Snowflake and Lightning.* And then that turned into, *Name her? Oh no. What am I supposed to name her?* And then:

Name ideas (for Snowflake):
Snowflake
Snow
Flake
Turkey Wing
Wing
Ghost
No, not Ghost.
But maybe . . . No. Hmm. Little No Richardson. And we can maybe nickname her No-No.

"Your dad told me y'all talked last night." Mom got the cereal and a bowl from the cabinet and set them on the counter.

"Yeah," I said, scanning the inside of the fridge.

Ketchup. Leftover veggies. Baking soda. I grabbed the milk and the orange juice.

"Wanna talk about it?" See? That's a mom.

I thought about if I wanted to talk about it as I poured cereal into the bowl, then milk onto the cereal. Did I want to talk about it? Did I have questions? Nope. Not really. My dad wasn't always my dad. I guess I get that. I mean, I wasn't always the fine-o albino. I used to be Lu with the thick glasses that made me look like I was part fish. Like I was a mermaid man. A man-maid. A merman. This was before Dad gave me some of his gold chains. Before the earrings. Before the fresh fit and the contact lenses. But now all that's fixed, and I'm me. So I guess as long as you try to fix the mess-ups, then . . . well . . . but my father's mess-ups messed other people's lives up. Big-time. Maybe that's different. I don't know.

But I can understand wanting to be cool.

Everybody can understand just wanting to be cool.

"Nah. Not really," this time out loud. I jammed a spoon into the bowl, shoveled cereal into my mouth.

Mom nodded but looked at me to make sure I was good. Make sure there were no cracks. No flash of water in my eyes. "Okay, well then, as soon as you finish breakfast, we can get to work," she said, flipping through the pages of her list. This was a list of all the people who'd placed orders with her for fruit art gifts, which meant she (we) had to first go grocery shopping for enough fruit to last the rest of the week, then come back to make the . . . thing—whichever one was being delivered today—and deliver it. And because I was out of school, I pretty much had to be her assistant.

"Let's see here. The first order is for a man named"— she double-checked the paper—"Charles Ringwald. Hmm. Sounds like a distinguished gentleman." Distinguished is my mother's way of saying fancy, and whenever she says it, she makes her mouth do this weird frown thing, but it's not a sad frown, it's a . . . *distinguished* frown. "Celebrating an anniversary. The message says, 'Dear Picasso of Produce, can you please deliver a gift to my friend Charles? I'd love it to look like a cowboy. And for the message on the card, I'd like it to say, *Four years ago you saved our lives. And we'll always be grateful. Love, Terri and Castle.*'"

"Terri and *who?*" I almost choked on my cereal.

"Says . . . Castle," my mother repeated, squinting at the paper.

"That's Ghost! I mean, maybe there's another Castle out there, but I'm pretty sure that's Ghost."

"Ghost . . ."

"From the team."

"His mama named him Castle?"

"Yeah. I mean, you rather she named him Ghost?"

"Good point." My mother took a sip from her cup, swallowed, and *aah*'d dramatically. "Well, this is business, so don't go running your mouth about it to him." She read farther down the letter, mumbling to herself about the time this cowboy needed to be delivered. "Okay, between noon and three . . . yadda yadda yadda . . . son's gonna be there," she read on, before rolling the paper up.

"He's gonna be there?" I asked. He, being Ghost.

"Look, you know my rule. People give gifts for all kinds of reasons, and it's none of our business. Our business is to deliver and move on. Got it?" She pointed at me.

"Of course. Sheesh."

"Good." She tapped her chin with the paper tube, thinking. "Now . . . a cowboy . . ."

In the spring and summer, my mother skips the normal grocery store and goes all the way across the city, over where Sunny lives, to an outside market where people sell fruit they say came from their own farms. But ain't no farms around here, so the way I see it, we might as well just go to the regular store, where I can at least pretend the shopping cart is a scooter. At the so-called farmers' market, where the so-called farmers (though they never even look like farmers) sell fruit and veggies, and all kinds of other stuff, there was an old lady named Granny who was selling cookies, which seemed weird because those ain't grow on no farm. Other folks were selling like fifteen different kinds of honey and ten kinds of peanut butter. Some dude who looked like he was all hair and no skin was selling drinks made of blended-up grass, which seems silly because I don't think you supposed to drink grass, and if you wanted to, you definitely shouldn't have to pay for it.

We grabbed a few watermelons, some cantaloupe, and some of the ones that's green on the inside. Some strawberries, grapes, bananas, a bunch of kiwi, and a few different kinds of oranges, because there are a bunch of different versions of orange, but they all pretty much taste like orange. Navel oranges got the belly button, but they don't have seeds. Valencia oranges got seeds, thin skin, and all the juice. The blood orange is red on the inside. The tangerine is called a tangerine even though it's still an orange. Same as the clementine. And the grapefruit. I don't really know if that's true or not, but it seems like a grapefruit is just a nasty-tasting orange.

We got everything we needed from the same

lady—a woman named Frankie, who had the dirtiest fingernails I ever seen in my whole life, and a faded T-shirt that said YOU ARE WHAT YOU EAT.

When we got home, we unloaded everything, then got to work.

Mom has made it all. I'm talking about baby cribs out of watermelon rind, cars out of cantaloupe. She's made solar systems using grapes and cherries and kiwi for planets, and turned slices of apples into small canoes. One time she made peach pits—the part in the middle of the peach—look like a bunch of little brains. That one was for a Halloween party at a brain doctor's house, so it was a double whammy.

Today, a cowboy. Well, not really a cowboy. See, even though people ask for certain things, my mother pretty much gives them what she feels like she can make, which is sometimes the thing they asked for, and . . . sometimes something close to the thing they asked for. So, a cowboy *hat*. I mean . . . same thing, right? It's related, and it's definitely the part that matters most. Without the hat, a cowboy's just a dude. Plus, cowboys call themselves cowboys and don't never be with a cow. So, the way I see it, my mom can call a cowboy hat a cowboy, if she feels like it.

"Okay, so you already know what I need you to do."

Mom laid out the fruit on the counter, round things rolling all over the place.

"Peel the oranges." I said it flat, in the same voice I use when Coach asks us what the best do.

"Because you're the Orange Master," she sang, pulling knives from the drawer. "But first, wash your hands. I know it's early, but your fingers probably been all up in your nose, and who knows where else." She only said that because before I was the Orange Master, I was the Booger Master, but that was a long time ago and she just won't let it go.

The plan was simple. First she cut the rind off the watermelon, cutting the round parts into straight parts, like turning a circle into a square. Or in this case, a rectangle. Then she cut chunks out the sides of the rectangle, like . . . *hmm* . . . turning it into an upside-down T, but an upside-down T if the stem part of the T is short and fat. This probably ain't making no sense. So . . . let me see. Just . . . she cut the watermelon into the shape of a cowboy hat, okay? Just take my word for it. Then, what I did, after peeling a few oranges, was pull them into slices and put them in a bowl.

"Toothpick," my mother said, like a surgeon asking for the surgery knife. I handed her one from the container. She grabbed one of the slices from the bowl, stabbed it with the skinny wooden spear, then jammed it into the hunk of watermelon.

"Another one," she commanded. I handed her another toothpick. The thing about this process is that I honestly never knew what she was doing or how she was going to turn whatever fruit we had on the table into some kind of masterpiece. It usually happened just like it was happening this time. She'd tell me what I was supposed to cut or peel the skin off—usually oranges—and then she'd say random words like, "toothpick" or "honey," or my favorite, which is "wallawallabingbang," which she only said when she was done and happy with her creation. Because my mom thinks it's funny. Because my mom is . . . my mom.

This went on—the toothpicking and the toothpick passing—and the orange slices I'd prepared (prepared always makes me feel like I did more than just peel and split) created the band of the cowboy hat. I ain't even know cowboy hats had bands around them. Like the ribbon part that's usually on smooth hats worn by smooth people. Suit hats, not cowboy hats. But I don't really know nothing about cowboys, so, whatever. Maybe they do. Mom had also taken grapes and attached them along the border of the watermelon block, which I guess would be the brim of the hat. I ain't think cowboy hats had decoration around the brim. I ain't think cowboys were so . . . fancy. But mothers know a lot of stuff about a lot of stuff, so when she yelled, "Wallawallabingbang!" I knew cowboy hats could be fancy. At least in her world.

"That's it?" I asked, sizing up the art. I tilted my head a little, hoping that it would look more cowboy-y if I checked it out from a side view.

"That's it. Ain't she something?"

"*She* look like a . . . one of the ones I see . . . a Mexican kind—"

"A sombrero? Nope. Definitely not. Too small." She shook her head and pointed to a picture of a woman on the windowsill, just above the sink. My mother loved this lady. Her name was Frida. Mom always said the lady Frida also made lightning. Through art. In the photo Frida was standing next to this big dude and was wearing a sombrero. I've been seeing this picture my whole life and never even noticed it. "*That's* a sombrero." She picked the picture up, examined it, glanced at the watermelon hat, then back to the picture, and added, "Well . . . maybe a little. But still, this is a cowboy hat for the . . . *confident* cowboy." She set the picture down, then turned to me. "Listen, it's artistic expression. So . . . let's just box it up, and go, 'kay?"

There's a tradition my mom and me have when delivering her fruit masterpieces. On the way, we listen to her music, which is old music, and on the way back we listen to my music, which is good music. On this trip, going, it was Bobby Brown. He got a song called "Roni" that my mother loves, that I think is so funny, because this dude, Bobby, just be calling this girl that he says he loves a "Tenderoni," which I think is such a stupid name. Seriously. Like . . . what? So whenever Mom be singing it, I just change out Tenderoni with Macaroni or Pepperoni. It makes her so mad.

"You ruining this song for me, Lu. Do you know your dad and I danced to this on our first date *and* at our wedding?" She turned the volume down just low enough to make sure I could hear her, and she could still hear the song.

"If Dad called you Tenderoni, why would you go out on a second date with him? That's like calling you Turkey Wing," I explained. *"'Oh, oh, if you find a Turkey Wing that is right for youuuuu,'"* I sang, pretending to be a lover boy like Bobby Brown apparently was.

"You too young to understand."

"Okay, so . . . you want me to call girls Tenderonis? Tenderoni and cheese? Tenderoni salad? Tenderoni sounds like cooked macaroni. Matter fact, Dad told me I could name my new little sister."

"I know. So . . ." She checked her mirror, slapped her blinker on.

"So what if I went with Tenderoni? Tenderoni Richardson. Rolls off the tongue."

"Okay, Lu. Okay, okay. You win," she said, changing the station. Next up, a tune called "My Prerogative."

"*Ugh*. What . . . is . . . he . . . *talking* about?"

"You know what . . ." Mom sucked her teeth and turned the radio off.

We drove down the boulevard, cutting through neighborhoods, the street that I'd become so used to running on Thursdays when the Defenders did our long run. Eventually we turned in to Glass Manor.

"Says it's right around here," Mom said, slowing down in front of . . . *not* the house of a *distinguished gentleman*.

"Right here?"

Mom checked her paperwork. Then checked the GPS. "That's what it says. Right here."

It was a corner store. The sign above it read in faded

paint: MR. CHARLES'S COUNTRY STORE, which I thought was funny because we don't live in the country. But we were delivering a cowboy hat that we made from fruit grown on some lady named Frankie's farm, so . . . maybe this Mr. Charles knew something I ain't know. I'd been holding the cowboy hat in one of the plastic boxes my mother uses—stickered and ribboned—the whole ride to make sure the potholes ain't ruin it. They didn't. My mother's car was a different story.

"You got this, runner?" my mother asked, putting the car in park and leaning over to peer out the passenger window to make sure we were at the right place. What she meant by "You got this, runner?" was, *Lu, get your butt out and deliver this to the door*. I was the runner. Not just on the track, but off the track too, back and forth from the car to all the lucky customers who were the proud recipients of fancy-looking fruit . . . things. Bowls. Baskets. Fruit . . . pieces. Not pieces of fruit, but *master*pieces of fruit.

"Of course," I said, opening the door. I always say *of course* because I know I really don't got no choice. And I've met, or at least said hello to, some strange people. Snake milkers, who are these people who take venom out of snake fangs so it can be used for medicine, which is a medicine I don't never want to take. Or this lady who was a professional snuggler, which would be the perfect job for somebody like Sunny. Or a dog-food taster—a man who tested dog food by tasting it to make sure it was good . . . for dogs. Yeah. But this time I *wanted* to be the runner, because I just knew Ghost was gonna be there.

"Lu." My mother tugged on the back of my shirt as I was trying to get out of the car. "Remember, this is work time. This ain't about your friend." Another reminder.

I nodded. One foot out of the car.

"And Lu, remember to smile."

"I know." Two feet out.

"Oh, and say, good after—" she went on, but the "noon" in "afternoon" got snipped by the slamming door.

The store was wide open, and I walked right in, mouth also wide open. Big (fake) smile, ready to hit the stage and play myself, with *Good afternoon, my name is Lu, and I have a package for Mr. Charles Ringwald, from Picasso of Produce.* And right before I broke into it, I caught a familiar face in the corner of my eye.

I turned, looked.

Stuck. Swallowed. Stick in throat.

Ghost. Standing next to who I wished was a ghost.

Kelvin.

No.

No. No. No. No. No. No. Kelvin. *NO! NO!*

   Not him! NOT HIM!

Kelvin Jefferson. Or, Smellvin Kelvin, as I called him, but only when he wasn't around or when I was talking under my breath. He was in the same class with me every year. And because of this stupid idea teachers be having about doing *everything* in alphabetical order, as if that's the only way to be organized, I always ended up sitting right next to him. Yes, even though the *J* in Jefferson is far away from the *R* in Richardson, it was just my luck the only person with a last name between those letters, Corey Moore, had bad hearing and did better sitting in the front of the class. So, that left Smellvin's *J* sitting right next to my *R*. Which basically means I was always in slap-on-the-back-of-the-head range. Always close enough to hear him whisper:

Yo, you look like a cotton ball dipped in white paint.

   Like milk. Like somebody supposed to pour you over cereal.

   Like grits with no butter.

   Like sugar.

Like a cloud with eyeballs.

Like vanilla ice cream with whipped cream on top.

Like the lines of a crosswalk before being walked on.

Like your face look like fake teeth.

Your whole body look like the palm of a hand.

Like a Q-tip.

Like cooked rice.

Like fresh snow.

Like a ashy elbow.

Like the moon if the moon had arms and legs. And ashy elbows.

Like soapsuds.

Yo, you look like spat-out toothpaste.

Like old tighty-whities, bleached.

Like bleach bleached.

Like a uncracked egg. And not the brown kind. The white kind.

Like a piece of paper with no lines and no ink.

Like a whole bucket of baby powder.

Like a ghost that God brought back to life but still left as a ghost.

Yo, you look like something wrong with you.

Yo, you look like something wrong with you.

Yo, you look like something wrong.

Yeah. Seven years of Kelvin Jefferson. He used to scrape mud off the bottom of his sneakers and smear it on me and say, *Look, I fixed you!* And when I tried to "fix" him back, when one day at recess, in the fourth grade, I finally was able to scream out *Smellvin!* and tell him that his breath smelled like he had a rotten tongue, like his teeth were made of mildew, like he ate scrambled poop for breakfast, like he tried to wash up in his own sweat, like he drank toilet water . . . with a straw. And he had all these dark spots on his arms and legs. Purple and blue. Told him it looked like God was trying to make a leopard but halfway through changed his mind and decided to make a loser. When I finally got the nerve to hit him with all the rapid-fire heat I'd been storing up, Kelvin squared up, puffed out, balled up his fists. (Surprise!) And when he did that, I stepped back, lifted the orange I was holding—I'd saved it from lunch—cocked it back like a pitcher, and fast-balled it at his ugly face. *BLAP!* Snot and pulp all over the place. Fool started crying like a little baby.

Okay, okay, okay. I'm lying.

That part about the orange, that ain't happen. I mean, it did, but only in my mind.

Kelvin Jeff . . . er . . . son. See, here's the thing about Kelvin Jefferson. He big for his age. *Too* big. It don't even really look like he was born, but instead was built, put together in some kind of blockhead bully factory. Assembled. Like there was a conveyor belt that just screwed on his arms and legs. Something like that. Dude stands like a capital T. That's how I knew them purple and blue spots weren't bruises, or nothing like that. Couldn't have been, because nobody was big enough to bruise Kelvin. Nobody. So when I tried to zing him back—it was more like, *zing zing zing zing zing!*—he squared up on me.

And . . . I . . . dropped the orange and ran. Got *ghost*. Zoomed around the monkey bars, and back and forth across the basketball court. I dodged him as he cannonballed toward me, weaving through the swings, bumbling across the field like some kind of corny—but scary—fairy-tale troll. And when we got back to class, I sat on the edge of my chair with only half of a half a butt cheek actually on the seat part. The rest of me was just kinda hovering there, my face turned to the side so one eye could always be on him, waiting for school to be over. And as soon as it was out . . . I was out. Jetted. *Pyewn!* He tried to keep up but stumbled over his clunky feet in the hallway. I heard it but didn't see it. Wasn't about to turn around. Just kept pumping out of school, through the bus lines and carpool kids, past the crossing guards, slicing right through their *stop* whistles, off school property, through Barnaby Terrace, home.

When I got to my house, my mother asked me what was wrong, and I wasn't about to tell her, *Kelvin Jefferson*. I couldn't.

I know what you thinking. Bullies should be snitched on, especially if you don't feel like you can back them down. And honestly, I agree. But in that moment, I'm thinking about me, about how my name would go from Lucas *Mucus*—which is what he called me—to Snot as soon as my mother showed up to the school all mom'd out, ready to see who's "teasing her baby." She'd probably be wearing her mommiest of mom clothes, like them sneakers she swear cool, even though I keep telling her they not. And then she say they comfortable. And then I say that's why they ain't cool. And then I'd have to get called out of class over the intercom, and then Kelvin and I would have to sit in the principal's office, or worse, the nurse's office, and talk about our feelings, and I would be okay with talking about mine because they were being hurt every single day, but he would probably go back to class and tell everybody I was crying and that I snitched on him and that my mother with the busted shoes came to beg him to be nice to me. *The fly boy ain't nothing but a cry boy. Wah wah wah.*

And I ain't need that.

So I told her I was just . . . practicing.

"Practicing for what?" She looked at me, and I could tell she was looking for the lie.

I said the only thing I could come up with at the time. "Um, I'm practicing . . . for . . . sports." Sports? Just . . . sports? Who says that? Me. That's who. What can I say? What could I have said back then other than that? That I was practicing being out of breath? Practicing not getting crunched by a dude twice my size and having my new chains—my dad's chains—snatched? So yeah, I said *sports*.

The thing is, the only sport my mother could think of that involved no physical contact (because she wasn't having that . . . and neither was I) was . . . running. Track.

So, here I am. A runner, because I was scared to fight Kelvin freakin' Jefferson.

Anyway, this the first year me and Kelvin ain't have class together. Or school together. Well, we did, but only for half the year. He stopped coming right before the track season. Just . . . disappeared. Some people said he quit school and went to work. He definitely could be mistaken for a grown man, but for real for real, his grades were too good to quit school. He was a dummy, but he wasn't no dummy. Some people said he was in juvie. But I ain't believe that either. Other people said they heard teachers talking about he had stuff going on at home, and whenever people say *stuff going on at home*, they mean bad stuff. And because of that Kelvin had to move in with his grandfather. That made more sense.

All I know is I was glad he was gone. Meant I ain't have to always be looking over my shoulder, worried he was gonna get me. Which is why I was so surprised (scared) to now, all of a sudden, see him standing right in front of me, in this corner store.

Un-gone.

I swallowed again, this time forcing down the *Good* and hacking up, "aft . . . er . . . noon . . . um . . . ," turning toward the man behind the counter. He was a funny-looking old guy with a white waterfall of hair flowing from his head. His face was friendly, but his skin was loose like a trash bag with a basketball in it. *Get it together. Start over.* "Um, sir. Good, good afternoon." I tried to save the smile, but it was too late. It also might've been too late to save myself. I glanced back at Kelvin, who was looking at me with the same wild look I was probably giving him.

"What you say?" the man behind the counter, who I figured was Mr. Charles, asked. It wasn't until then that I realized how loud it was in the store. There was a TV behind the counter showing something old, something black-and-white, something involving horses.

"What you doing here, cream filling?" Kelvin said, his head cocked, his eyes going small.

"How . . . what . . . *you* doing here?" I shot back, my eyes going big.

"Y'all know each other?" Ghost said. He was coming toward me with his hand out. He was dusty, and his T-shirt was spotted with sweat. Both of theirs were, but Kelvin always looked like that.

"Yeah . . . unfortunately," I muttered, slapping Ghost's hand, but it was so loud in that place, he probably ain't hear me.

"What you say?!" the man behind the counter shouted again.

"Oh . . ." I turned back to what I was supposed to be doing, which was delivering a cowboy hat made of fruit. "I have a delivery for Mr. Charles."

"I'm Mr. Charles, but I didn't order nothing, unless

you got extra toilet paper, because I'm missing some of my toilet paper order." He pressed his fingertip to a piece of paper on the counter.

"No, no, we found the rest of it in a different box," Ghost said, brushing dust from his T-shirt.

"What?!"

"I said, we found it! We found the TP!" Ghost shouted.

"You found the TV? It's right here. Been here for years. It's the toilet paper we're looking for, but don't worry, I think maybe this young man has brought it." Mr. Charles smiled. I was so confused. Mr. Charles turned back to me, leaned over the counter. "That was a joke, son. I know you aren't delivering toilet paper."

"No, he's not," Ghost chimed in, grabbing the plastic box. "This is a gift from me and my mom."

And then *my* mom hit the horn. She was probably wondering what was taking me so long, and I knew that I only had a few seconds before she came through the door, and then I'd be even more freaked out. She was wearing her comfy shoes. The mom ones.

"Um . . . I gotta go," I said, setting the card on the counter. "Ghost, I'll get at you later." And, I, the runner, ran back to the car.

"You all right?" Mom asked as I basically dove back into the passenger seat, my heart booming like rap bass.

"Yeah." I glanced over at the store again. The old man, Mr. Charles, had come around the counter. He was hugging Ghost.

"What took you so long?"

"I was . . . talking to Ghost. Not about the cowboy hat. Just . . . talking." I darted my eyes at her. Shrugged. Swallowed. Smirked. Then put my eyes forward. I was definitely a little shook. A lot shook. And she was looking at me, grilling the side of my face with her eyeballs of fire. "Time for some music," I said, uncomfortable, turning the radio on, and immediately jumping to the station that plays good music. Not music about . . . prerogatives or piranhas or whatever they be talking about in my mother's songs.

"Oh boy," Mom groaned, finally pulling away from the store. "Time for some of that *boompity bump bump, yeah, yeah, yeah, ah, ah, woo, woo, grrr, skit skrrrt* music you love so much. Let's hope it don't make me nauseous." She bobbed her head ridiculously hard, to be silly. "Use your words, child! Use your *words!*" she yelled at the radio.

I tried. Before. To use my words. Even though my

mother wasn't talking about me, that's what I wanted to say. I tried before to use my words. And my words almost got me crushed. By Kelvin Jefferson. I always thought the thing about lightning bolts was that they were electric enough to never have to speak. I thought they could just strike. Could just set fire. And disappear.

6

A NEW NAME FOR HURDLE:
Blur (or Blurdle or Aaron)

Mantra. That just means something you tell yourself all the time. Like, a pep talk you say to get yourself going. At least that's what it is for me. My mother taught me about mantras when I was a little boy. Every night before bed I had to say, *I am* . . . and then add good stuff to it. Like, *I am* . . . happy. *I am* . . . smart. Stuff like that. But as I got older, I flipped it. Added new things that I've stuck with and say every day before I go to practice or to a meet or to school. Just a way to build me up. Get me hype. Like preparing for battle. And after bumping into Smellvin Kelvin, I needed my mantra. Bad.

I am

The man.

The guy.

The kid.

The one.

The only.

The Lu.

Lucky Lu.

Lookie Lu.

Lu the Lightning Bolt.

I repeated it a few times, staring in the mirror, trying to calm myself down. Trying to quiet down the slamming sound in my brain. Trying to unscrew the doorknob stuck in my throat. *I am the man. The guy. The kid.*

Over and over again.

The one. The only.

Repeating it, almost like whispering it to myself, hoping that the part of myself I can't see believes it. Like there's another me in there that I'm talking to.

It's part of a whole routine I got. I say my mantra and then I put my sunscreen on, rubbing it into my legs and my arms and my shoulders and neck. Rubbing it into my face. And it's thick, so I always gotta rub pretty hard so that it all goes all the way into my skin.

Today I rubbed my face, first small circles, then bigger circles, the white lotion globby like some kind of glue.

I'm the man. The guy. The kid.

Rubbing my face harder, thinking about Kelvin. His block head. *The one.* His stank breath. *The only.* His wack jokes. Rubbing the lotion in even harder, now using my whole hand, mashing my cheeks, squishing, wrinkling my forehead, staring at myself in the mirror. Ugly. The white on top of the white. The brown nowhere to be found. *The Lu.* Harder. *Lucky Lu.* Harder! *Lucky, lucky,*

> *lucky,*

> > *lucky,*

> > > *LUCKY,*

> > > > *LUCKY . . .*

I rubbed and rubbed until all the lotion was gone and my skin started to burn like it was gonna roll off, and my eyes started to go wet. *Lucky . . . me.*

I was just about to take my contacts out and clean them—part of the ritual—but in this moment decided to just leave them in and use eyedrops. Quick. A drop or two in each, then clean up the dripping tears, which weren't *tears* but were . . . eyedrops. Eyedrops. Because that's what happens when you put eyedrops in. Only people who got dry eyes know that. Or people with contacts. I got . . . contacts. Been wearing them since forever, because the other thing about being albino is that it also messes with the goodness in your eyes. It took my brown *and* gave me this thing called hyperopia, which ain't got nothing to do with being hyper, even though that's what it sounds like. It basically just means that whatever is right in front of me is blurry. Like . . . *real* blurry. And I can only see things when they are far away. I know—makes no sense. Most people call this farsighted, but when it's as bad as mine, it gets a fancy name.

That's why I was saying I used to be "Lu with the thick glasses" when I was little. My mom thought it was cute. A little boy with magnifying glasses strapped to his face. She still do, and sometimes I catch her looking through old photos of me wearing big goggle-looking specs, like I was about to go scuba diving or something. But when you get older and you a lightning bolt, and you got on glasses thicker than the back of Coach's neck, you figure out how to not wear them, and instead how to stick smaller versions of them lenses right on your eyeballs. That sounds like something Sunny would say. Point is, wearing contact lenses is just part of my life. A part I've been able to hide pretty well. Until I got to practice today.

I was still feeling a little funny after seeing Kelvin—really I was feeling so so so mad because I thought the dude was gone!—and had a bunch of stuff I wanted to ask Ghost, like, how he knew him. Were they friends? Did he know how much that dude sucked and that he's the only reason I started running in the first place? But when I got to the park, Ghost wasn't really in the mood to talk. He was sitting on the bench—the bench we always sat on before practice—Patty and Sunny standing over him.

"It just came today?" Patty asked as I walked up. She glanced at me, did a shiver thing with her head, a signal that something was wrong.

"What's going on?" I asked.

"Ghost got a letter today," Sunny said.

"A letter?"

"From his dad," he explained.

Ghost stood up, folded the paper in his hand. He glanced at me, his eyes glassy with the feelings he was holding back. "Today's the day. Was the day. Four years ago . . . he . . ." Ghost paused, took a breath. "Today—"

It hit me.

"Is . . . the anniversary." I cut him off, and then felt bad for cutting him off, but he nodded like he was relieved. "It was in the note," I added. I was just trying to figure it all out. "But . . . the cowboy hat . . . what does that old man have to do . . ." I was trying to say it but couldn't figure out how to ask the question without sounding (more) like a jerk.

Patty looked at me like I was sounding like a jerk.

Sunny looked at me the same way, which meant I must've been *really* sounding like a jerk.

"Sorry. I ain't mean to . . . I just—"

"It's cool," Ghost said. "That old man saved our lives. He hid my mom and me in his storage room." He slapped the folded paper up against his head, as if he was trying to convince the words to go into his brain. "And now, here my father go sending me this. First time I've heard from this dude since it all went down."

"What it say?" I asked, dropping my duffel.

"It says mind your business, dummy!" Patty barked. Ghost chuckled a little.

"Maybe that's what I'll write back to him," he joked.

"I can help with that, if you want," Sunny offered, all nice.

"Thanks. I mean, maybe." He slapped the paper rectangle in his other hand and turned back to me. "It just says that he's sorry and . . . whatever." Ghost tried to get himself together. "Whatever, whatever, whatever.

I'm fine. Let's just get on the track before Coach comes. I'm good." We all gave Ghost a look. A look like my mother gives me. Looking for cracks. "Seriously. I'm *good*. Come on, before he starts trippin'."

"Yeah, and don't nobody need to hear all that today," I said, remembering my role as co-captain, which Coach said was to lead by example. And even though we made it to the track before being told to be there, that ain't stop Coach from yapping anyway. He was Coach. And that's what Coach does.

"Okay. Today is Tuesday," Coach announced. "Do I need to tell you all what we're doing?"

"No."

"Do I need to tell you all why we're doing it?"

"No."

"Do I need to explain what the best do?"

"No."

"What do the best do?"

"The best never rest."

"What do the best do?" He put his hand to his ear.

"The best never rest!"

Coach nodded, shot his eyes at Whit, who nodded back.

"That's what I'm talking about. Let's get to work."

It was time for our stretches, and because I was

already bubbling up inside from earlier, I kept my mouth shut when Aaron started counting off and doing his usual captain crap. Crap-tain Aaron. His stupid voice counting, calling out left and right, this stretch and that stretch in that fake think-he-somebody voice. But I kept it cool. Leading by example. (I know I wasn't the only person annoyed by this dude.) Until it was time to run our warm-up laps, and he tried me. Aaron bumped me, then sniffed all in the air, talking about something smells like burnt plastic.

He was talking about me. All the sunscreen.

"That's you, Lu?" he said. But he already knew it was me and was trying to be funny. He'd been smelling it all season, and everyone knew I *had* to wear it or the sun would literally cook my skin. But today he felt like calling me out. But he ain't know it was the wrong day for that.

After his slick comment, he broke out running before I could say anything, and called out to the team, "Keep pace with me!" He always set the pace. It made him feel like some kind of big man, like he was the boss of us. I could just tell. And honestly, I was over people acting like they were my boss. Like they were bigger and better than me. Like they could say and do anything to me. I hadn't even seen Kelvin since

December, but seeing him in that corner store brought it all back. His dumb jokes were still with me, in me, wrapped around me like skin. And now, here come this show-off, Aaron.

So . . . I jetted out in front of him. "Come on, Defenders. Keep up. Let's go!" I called out.

I was a good five paces in front of Aaron when he barked, "Yo, what you doing?"

"No talking, Aaron. Just keep up!" I shot over my shoulder. Burnt plastic. *Yeah, okay.* I could hear Aaron's steps go faster, and a few seconds later he was on my side, pumping his arms wider than he needed to, inching closer and closer to me. He was trying to chicken-wing me. Trying to elbow me.

"Chill," I said, as we rounded the bend. But he wouldn't. Kept cranking his arms wild. But he ain't faster than me. He wishes he was, but he's not. So I hit the jets on him. Jumped up ten paces. And again, he sped up to keep up. Couldn't catch me, but I could hear his feet slapping the track, faster and faster. So I boosted on him one more time. Now we were running at almost full speed, until all of a sudden I felt something on the back of my heel. It was the bottom of his shoe. He clipped me, and my right leg locked up. I torpedoed to the ground. Hard. But I was only down for a second.

"Yo, what's your problem?" I bounced up, got in his face, my body stinging from the crash. The rest of me stinging from . . . everything else.

"*My* problem?" Aaron barked back, breathing hard. He inched closer. "You the one with the problem."

"I'm just trying to do my job, but I can't because you such a hater." I matched his inch closer with my own.

"You better chill out, newbie. I earned my spot as the captain of this team. I worked for that position. I ain't have to play *dress up* to get it." Aaron reached over and grabbed my gold chains and flipped them up into my face.

And . . . *boom.* I lost it. Charged him, tried to put every word I could think of—every snap, every fry, every flame I could throw at him—into my arms and pushed him as hard as I could. But he ain't fly like I expected. Matter fact, he barely went anywhere. Just took a few steps back. Smirked. Then charged me and shoved *me* with his whole body, and *I* flew to the ground. Again. By this time, everyone had gathered around us to try to stop the drama. Curron and Mikey were pulling Aaron—laughing—away, and Patty and Ghost were helping me up.

"Shut up!" I shouted at Aaron. Trying to pull away from Ghost and Patty, I said, "Get . . . off me!" to them.

"You better relax, Snow White," Aaron taunted. "Let your dwarves help you." Now Ghost let go of my arm and started marching toward Aaron, but Chris blocked him.

"It's not worth it, Ghost," Chris warned.

"I don't even know why you would defend him, Ghost," Aaron continued. "*Especially* after how he played you out when you first joined the team. Remember? Trashed you because of your shoes. Because he was *scared* you were better than him."

"Shut up!" I shouted again, my voice roller-coastering. "Shut up, before . . . before . . . I make you shut up." I wiped my eyes fast, then wiped them again faster.

"What is going on?!" Coach and Whit, finally realizing what was happening, made their way across the field to where we were.

"He clipped me!" I yelled.

"I set the pace, like I always do. And for some reason, he tried to take over and basically burned the whole team out." Aaron's voice was calm. Like none of it was affecting him.

"Yeah, but that's because I'm sick of his mouth, Coach."

"And I'm sick of yours, Lu." Coach shot his eyes at

Aaron. "*And* yours." He gave us both growl eyes. "*Really? Really?* Y'all do this the week of the championship, and call yourselves captains?" Coach slapped his hands to his cheeks, let out a heavy exhale. "Know what, I don't have time for this. Mikey, Patty, y'all captains for the rest of the day." Then he turned back to us. "You two, give me two more warm-up laps, and since y'all can't seem to figure out a good pace, I'll set one—full speed. And when you're done, don't even think about asking for water or anything. Captains." Coach saluted us and walked away.

After the second warm-up—I think I got him by a step or two—Aaron joined Mikey and the other four-hundred runners. Everyone else had already split into their groups to work on handoffs, starts, strides, pacing. And I went and stood over by the hurdles. Coach had set a few up for me before practice. Only four, instead of the ten I had to jump in the actual race. I waited for him while he talked to Sunny, who was standing in his throwing circle with a finger in the air. Coach shook his head, then came jogging over to me.

"Sorry about that," he said. "Trying to get Sunny to understand how to adjust for the wind. Finally got him throwing straight, and the last thing I need is for the wind to carry the discus too far to the left or right and take one of y'all out like he almost did a few weeks back."

"Yeah," I said, not worrying about the wind at all. Felt pretty good to me. Especially since I was out of breath and sweating. Don't nothing feel better in the summertime than when breeze hits sweat.

"Before we get started, do we need to talk about what happened back there with you and Aaron?"

"No," I huffed, still trying to catch my breath.

"Yes. We do." Coach caught me off guard with that one. "And we don't have a lot of time, so I'm gonna make this quick. You two are exactly alike. You're just like him."

"No . . . I ain't." *Breathe. Breathe.* I ain't know what Coach was smoking, but he needed to quit. Me? Like Aaron? Get outta here. Aaron ain't got a ounce of lightning. He ain't even close.

"Oh yeah, you are. That's why I made you co-captain. He's like your pretend big brother."

"He . . . only one year older than me, Coach. So . . . nah." I was trying to get my breathing under control. In through the mouth, out through the nose. In through the mouth, out through the nose.

"Okay, okay. I'll leave it alone, but just remember

I told you that. And if I see any more fighting . . ." Coach didn't finish his sentence. And he ain't need to.

"Now, moving on to the next topic. How you feeling after our talk yesterday?"

"I'm . . . fine."

"You fine, but are you *ready*?"

I mean, at the moment I was tired. I just sprinted eight hundred meters and now he talking all this Aaron stuff, and about jumping hurdles. A lot to take in. But I needed to be ready. I had to be ready. I was gonna jump, I mean, hurdle the hurdles. That sounds silly. But whatever. I was doing it.

I took my place on the line, my chest burning, legs pulsing like they had hearts in them.

"Remember, get up quick, and lead with the knee," Coach coached.

Lead with the knee. Got it. *Get up quick. Lead with the knee. Breathe. Breathe.* And then . . .

Badeep!

The whistle blew and I took off, the first hurdle in front of me, and just as I got up on it, a gust of wind came whooshing at me, kicking up all kinds of dust from the side of the track and smacking it in my face. In my eyes. I tried to slow up in time but couldn't and ran right into the first hurdle.

I slapped my palms to my face, and heard Coach running over to me.

"You okay?"

"*Argh*. I'm fine, I'm fine," I said, using the heels of my hands to scrub my eyes. They felt glued shut by all the grit. "It's in my eyes." I walked over to the fence, scrubbed my eyes some more, mainly to try to get the sting to chill out, and to make my eyes water and to wash out whatever I could. But it wasn't working. My eyes felt crunchy. Like, toasted over. So I had to do what I never did before. I had to take my contacts out.

"You wear contacts?" Coach sounded surprised.

"Yeah, and without them, I can't see nothing." I had one balancing on the tip of my finger and was pinching the other one from my eyeball. "I mean, I can see, but I got hyperopia."

"You got *what*?"

"Hyper . . . I can only see faraway stuff." Figured it was easier to just say it like that. With both contacts out, I flicked them toward the grass. They were ruined, but luckily, I had fresh ones at home.

"Just far away?" Coach was acting like he ain't believe me. Like he wanted to put me to the test. He stood in front of me. I knew that because I could see the blur of red from his shirt. "How many fingers am I holding up?" *Seriously?* I couldn't tell if he was trying to be funny or what.

"Seriously?" I asked, for real.

"Seriously."

I knew he had his fingers up—plus he said he did— but there was no difference between one or five, and honestly, Coach could've had seven fingers on one hand and I wouldn't have known the difference.

I stared. Stared. Stared. Squinted. Stepped back. Squinted. Stepped back a little more but hit the fence. Came a little closer. Squinted. Then finally, just . . . shrugged.

"Oh no." Coach's voice suddenly dropped into concern. And I dropped my head. "Head up," he snapped immediately. But I ain't lift it. "Lu, did you hear me?"

I lifted it. Not all the way, though. "What we gon' do? I can't lose another day of practice, Coach."

"Can you see *anything*? Like, would you be able to tell if there was a hurdle in front of you?"

"I could probably tell there was *something* in front of me, but not really a hurdle."

"So what *can* you see?"

I looked over across the field. Sunny licked his finger and put it in the air again. I could see that.

"Sunny." I looked down to the curve and could see Patty stretching her arm out, passing the baton. "And Patty." I looked opposite the straightaway and could see Ghost, squatting, positioning himself for takeoff. "I can see Ghost, too."

Coach turned around to see how far they all were. Then he walked back to the center of the track, rearranged the hurdle I'd knocked out of place. Stood at the top of the line and looked down.

"Come here." When I got over to where he was standing—walking like a zombie—he put his arm around me and turned me so that I was facing down the track. Told me to look down the line of hurdles. "What you see?"

Everything was a blur of gray and white and red and green, becoming hurdles and track and grass the farther down the line I got. The clearest part was the end. "I can see . . . down there."

Coach nodded. Even though at the moment his face looked more like clay than face, I could tell he was nodding. "The finish line."

Here was Coach's plan (get ready for this): to jump the hurdles blind. *Surprise!* His theory was, since the hurdles were scaring me—they weren't . . . okay, they were—now I didn't have to be scared because I couldn't really *see* that they were hurdles, even though I could tell that something was there for me to get over. And that if I just stayed focused on what I could see, which luckily for me was what was at the end of the race, I could jump the hurdles just based on timing. I know. The dumbest thing I ever heard too. But what was I supposed to say? He was Coach. And I am Lu. The man. The guy. The kid.

And this was for the championship.

He asked me if I was sure I wanted to try this.

"Do I got a choice?"

"You always have a choice," he said.

My choice was, yes. He explained that what he wanted me to do was count how many steps it took for me to get from the starting line to the first hurdle. He moved the hurdle out of the way, which looked like a blur moving a smaller blur. Kinda looked like when my science teacher, Mr. Rich, played a video of what cells look like. Coach grabbed his clipboard and set it down on the track in the exact spot the hurdle was. At least that's what he told me. I had to take his word for it.

"Sprint straight down the lane. Just count your steps, and stop when you hear the whistle," he explained.

Badeep!

I took off. *One-two-three-four-five-six-seven-eight-nine-ten-eleven-twelve.* And could feel the ground change when I stepped on the wood of the clipboard. Could hear it too.

Badeep!

"How many?"

"Twelve."

"Twelve," Coach repeated, grabbing me by the arm and walking me back up the track. "Okay, so twelve will get you to the first. The rest . . ." He smiled. "The rest is the waltz."

"The what?" I stopped walking.

"You remember the dance I made you and Ghost do earlier in the season, when Patty and Deja and all them were learning to run their relay?"

Of course. How could I ever forget? Coach clowned us in front of everybody just for cracking a few jokes about Patty. Had us slow dancing in front of the whole team. "Coach, I can't do that again."

"Not the dancing part. But the counting." Coach led me back down to the hurdles. Everything blurry. He stood between the first and second hurdle. "Between these two, there's . . . one-two-three." Then he moved down and stood between the second and third hurdle. The farther he got, the clearer he became.

"One-two-three. Three steps, see?" Then between the third and fourth, unblurring a little more, his nose and ears appeared on his face again. "One-two-three. And then . . . hurdle."

"One-two-three, hurdle," I repeated, trying to understand and deal with my weird half-blind world.

"That's it. You don't have to see the hurdle to know it's there. You'll feel it in your way. And sometimes timing is all you need to get over it." I could tell by the sound of his voice that he was trying to control the excitement from his own ridiculous theory. "Let's give it a shot."

Again, he started walking me back to the starting line, this time all the way, going on and on about how risky this was, which was a terrible way to get me gassed up to do it. But I had to try it. Had to. Not just for me, but for the team.

I got on the line. "Twelve steps to get to the first. Then, waltz the others," Coach (as a funny-looking cloud) reminded me one more time before slipping the whistle in his mouth.

Twelve to get to the first. Waltz to the end. Get up quick. Lead with the knee. Twelve steps to get to the first. Twelve steps to get to the first. Twelve . . .

Badeep!

One-two-three-four-five-six-seven-eight-nine-ten-eleven-twelve. Up!

I went over,

    clean,

        smooth,

            like a . . . Tenderoni. Or something. I can't explain it, but it felt amazing. So amazing that I forgot the waltz part and added an extra step in there and clipped the next hurdle. I crashed hard on the track—my third time today—and could hear everybody else suck air through their teeth, like a bunch of hissing snakes (that needed their venom removed).

"I'm okay, I'm okay!" I called out, rolling onto my back, then rocking up and hopping to my feet. I brushed myself off.

"You sure?" Coach asked, running over. His voice sounded sideways, which meant his face was sideways, which meant he was looking for something. And I knew exactly what he was looking for. He was trying to see if I was embarrassed. I ain't have to see him to know that.

"Yeah, I'm straight." I was. It felt good to make it over one. Blind.

Coach's voice had some smirk in it when he said, "Then back on the line."

➤

After a few more falls, and eventually some successful jumps over all four hurdles, practice—which felt more like football than track—was over.

I sat on the bench and waited for my mom. The bench was the safest place for me, since I couldn't see nothing. I watched everybody go in and out of focus, from teammates to talking smudges, drifting around me. Aaron was Aaron, but he was nothing but a smear of brown when he walked by. He ain't say nothing. Me neither.

Ghost sat next to me, and it was like sitting next to a real ghost. He ain't say too much either. Even though I could hear the different voices of my teammates all around, I could also hear the crackling sound paper makes when folded or unfolded. Knew it was coming from Ghost and remembered the stuff about his dad. The anniversary. It had been a tough day for the both of us.

"You good?" I asked, rubbing my knees. They were sore. Scraped up. Sunny had already left—his father was almost always on time—and Patty had her little sister, Maddy, on her back, over by the parking lot, which is how I was able to see her, and was slap-boxing Deja. Her whole relay team, Deja, Krystal, and Brit-Brat, had been messing with her after practice, calling her Captain Jones.

"*You* good?" Ghost said back, the paper sound now gone. "Aaron finally got to you, huh?"

"Ain't nobody worried about Aaron," I snapped. "I'm worried about these hurdles. Either way, I'm good. I can't see nothin', but I'm good."

"Can't see?"

"Nah. Got dirt in my contacts, they got all messed up."

"You wear contacts?" Ghost asked, just like Coach asked, and I immediately thought he was going to roast me. But instead he followed with, "Dude, you know how wild you gotta be to stick something on your eyeballs? I can't just be touching my own eyeballs, bro. That's . . . nah."

I laughed, still rubbing my knees. Rubbing rubbing rubbing. Not as hard as earlier when I was putting on my sunscreen, but still hard enough to maybe rub the pain out. "It ain't that bad." *And I ain't that wild.*

"So you can't see, for real?" he asked, and I immediately knew he was waving his hands in front of my face, because everybody do the same thing. Plus the constant flashes of brown were making me feel sick.

"Stop."

"Couldn't help it."

"Anyway, like I was saying about the hurdles. I should be ready for Saturday if I can just stay out of my own head, y'know?" Rubbing. Rubbing.

"Of course I know." I heard Ghost's bag zip. He patted me on the shoulder, told me he'd see me tomorrow, and started walking away.

"Uh . . . Ghost? Help me out, bro," I called out. "I can't see, remember?"

"Oh yeah." Ghost came back, grabbed me by the arm, and we headed toward the parking lot. The breeze had settled and was now just whispering around us.

"Hey, can I ask you something?" I looked ahead, could see my mother pulling in in the distance.

"As long as it ain't about my dad."

"It's not. It's about that dude you were with today in the store. The big guy," I said. "How you know him?"

"I don't. Just met him today. In the summertime I always help Mr. Charles do stock, and clean, and just take care of different things in the store. It's only a few times a week, but at least it gives me something to do during the day. Plus, Mr. Charles always puts a little chicken in my pocket." He stopped. "Don't tell Coach, 'fore he try to hit me for cab fare. Anyway, I went in today, and that dude was there helping out too. Mr.

Charles told me he just moved to Glass Manor. Not sure from where, because we ain't talk about nothing like that. Just . . . basketball. I told him I used to hoop, but not no more. And then he just, like, started going on about how he's nice on the court. Swear he going to the league. *That* dude—that *big* dude—thinks he's going to the NBA." There was giggle in Ghost's voice. "I wanted to be like *NFL maybe*, but I don't know him like that yet."

"Word," I said, dry, partly because I still couldn't believe Kelvin was working with Ghost, and a partly because . . . the NBA? Really?

"Yeah. He seems okay, though. His name—"

"Kelvin," I cut him off. "I know his name. I know him." *And I know he is not okay.*

"Yeah, I could tell. But the way you was looking at him made me think y'all had static or something."

"Hmm. Nah. Ain't no beef. He just . . ." Then I thought about who I was talking to. Ghost. My friend. And if there's one thing I knew about him, it's that he ain't play with bullies. I remember what he told us happened between him and that boy at his school who was talking about him, what was his name? Run for the Bolts. I can't remember but I know he got balled up by Castle Cranshaw, and I ain't want *that* Ghost to do nothing to Kelvin and get fired from his job. Plus, Kelvin is *big*. Ghost ain't. And I know Ghost can hold his own, but . . . against the smelly capital T? Nah. Not without some serious lumps. "Ain't no beef, man. Just wanted to know how you knew him. I used to go to school with him. That's all." I reached my hand out for a five and started zombie-walking to my mother's car.

"Hey, oh, Lu, before you bounce, can I ask *you* something right quick?"

I turned around, thinking it would probably be about what Aaron said about me teasing Ghost when we first met. I called his shoes—the mashed-up ones he had ruined by cutting the high-top part off so that he could use them as running shoes—Freeboks. Sikes. And honestly, for that, I'm lucky Ghost ain't thump me too. "Wassup?" I braced myself. Ghost's face now just a smear of peanut butter.

"How come y'all delivered a sombrero?"

"Oh." I shrugged. "It's called art."

7

A NEW NAME FOR DAD: You Gotta Be
Kidding Me! For Real for Real?

My mother always calls Wednesday "Hump Day."
Which is . . . terrible. I mean, seriously? Hump
Day? Um . . . wow. But the reason she calls it that
is because she says that if you can get through
Wednesday, you've gotten over the hump, and the
rest of the week is a breeze. But for me, Wednesday
couldn't have been no worse than Tuesday. Matter
fact, they should call Tuesday "Hill Day," because a
hill is bigger than a hump. Either that, or Lu's Day,
which when you say it, sounds like Lose Day, even
though I thought I had some possible winners when

I was thinking of my little sister's name before bed.

Newbie.
Magic.
Breeze.
Windy.
Dusty. (Still thinking about this one.)
Hurdle. (Spelled Herdle.)

And then it kinda drifted into

One.
Two.
Three.
Four.
Nine.
Ten.
Eleven.
Twelve.
S l e e p.
Morning. Hump Day.

And the other thing about Hump Day, especially when it comes to my mom's business, is that no matter what, she *only* makes camels with the fruit. Only.

Camels. That's it. She started doing this a while ago when business really got jumping to the point that it was too much for her to handle by herself (when I'm in school), and she was trying to figure out a way to slow it down. So she made up this rule that if anybody orders something to be delivered on a Wednesday, it was going to be a camel, no matter what. She was hoping that people just wouldn't make Wednesday orders and she'd have a day off to relax. And that's basically what happened.

I got up, ready for a chill day, figuring maybe her and me could catch a movie—Sunny always be recommending strange ones—or maybe I could rest my sore body before practice. But as soon as I hit the kitchen, Mom just spat, "It's a workday." She poured a half cup of coffee for herself. Put the pot down, while I opened the fridge and took out the milk like a well-choreographed dance. One-two-three. Coffee-fridge-milk.

"On . . . Hump Day?" I asked, confused by the fact that anyone would want a camel.

"Yep." She nodded slowly. "On Hump Day." She ain't sound too excited. She was probably bummed about having to work on what was almost always a day off, but the other thing was that my mother had never actually got a real order on Hump Day before, so now she had to figure out how she was going to make a camel out of fruit.

"What's the game plan?" I asked, curious about this myself.

Mom leaned against the counter, took a sip, thinking, thinking, thinking, then . . .

"Kiwi. All kiwi."

For the rest of the morning I was stuck peeling kiwi, which is nothing like peeling oranges but is way more of a surprise. See, when you peel an orange, the inside of the orange is also . . . orange. I mean, there's the stuff that holds it all together, but mainly it's just orange. But when you peel a kiwi, the fuzzy brown reveals a bright green mushiness that you would never know was there. It's like cracking open a coconut and finding a tennis ball inside. Wild. So I did that, over and over and over and over and over and over again. She must've had twenty of them. I peeled, she chopped. I peeled, she chopped. And after she had a mountain of little pieces of kiwi, the juice running all over the place, she took a few bananas and put them and the kiwi in a blender and blended it all up. I won't lie. This was one of the strangest things I'd ever seen her do, and the whole time she had that real serious look on her face, chewing on her bottom lip like she knew she was about to shock the world.

I don't know about the world, but she definitely shocked me, because the bananas turned the kiwi into a thick paste. Almost like some kind of clay. And it was the color of clay. No, worse. And she shook it out of the blender and then shaped it into a camel with her hands. And when she got it right—two humps—she stuck it in the freezer for like ten minutes. And it was during this ten minutes, my mother ran to the bathroom to puke.

When she was done, she came back in the kitchen like it ain't happen. And that's when I realized that putting contacts on your eyeballs was *really* nothing compared to throwing up and then right after you done, taking a camel, that happens to look like it's MADE OF THROW-UP, out the freezer.

I just watched her as she poked it gently, and once she saw that it had turned a little stiffer, she started taking the leftover skin from all the kiwis I peeled and began laying it on top of the kiwi-banana blend. *What . . . the?*

"Toothpick," she called, as usual. I handed her one, then another one, and another one. and she used them to tack the skin down. And before I knew it, the camel had fur.

We stood back to get a good look at it. "Not bad," I said. "But who is it going to?"

My mother checked the paper, then smiled. "Of course."

"What?"

She handed me the note, and then she picked the tray up and put the camel back in the fridge. It said:

> *To: Skunk*
> *Thanks for helping us, especially Patty, get*
> *over the hump. And please clean your car*
> *out.*
> *Love, Ms. Bev Jones*

Underneath the signature, it said:

> *Christina, please feel free to deliver this*
> *gift in the middle of the day because*
> *Skunk don't have a job.*

Skunk was Cotton's older brother, and he had been helping Patty's family out since her aunt, who takes care of her, broke her arm in a car accident. Cotton and Skunk lived with their grandma right around the corner from me, so instead of getting in the car and driving, I told my mom I would just walk it over there. I got dressed, slathered on some sunscreen—just a single coat; it was a short walk—while Mom boxed up the "art," finishing the packaging with the usual ribbon and sticker. I grabbed a small tangerine and stuffed it in the pocket of my sweatpants. Picked up the box with the camel in it and headed for the door.

The sun was shining and the neighborhood was alive with kids excited to be out of school. Some were sitting on porches eating ice cups, some drawing on the sidewalk with pieces of fat chalk or some limestones they stole from Ms. Clark. She always kept limestones around her flower beds even though her flowers were always dead. I was holding the camel steady, maneuvering down the block, trying not to bump into some random little kid or, even worse, trip over nothing, which is what always happens when you don't need it to. Like when you holding your mom's hard work in the form of a fruit camel that was paid for by your friend's mother as a gift to a dude who was the older brother of the girl you like but don't like . . . to like.

Eventually, I got to the corner, made the right, and started down the next block. Almost there. A few more steps. And.

Trip. *Of course.* Over nothing. *Of course.*

Stumble. Stumble stumble. Save. *Phew!*

Clap!   *Clap!*   *Clap!*   *Clap!*

"*Yoooo*, you almost played yourself, kid!"

That was Skunk. He was sitting outside on his front porch, a cigarette dangling from his mouth as he continued to clap for me. Clap at me. A little scraggly hair dog sat next to him. The dog looked exhausted, as if it had worked a hard day. Or had been jumping hurdles. Or had been smoking cigarettes. The dog's name is Stinky Butt. Skunk's had him forever. "Almost lost your whole life out here," Skunk dragged the joke on. His voice was squeezed, almost choked, as he blew the smoke out, then dabbed the cig butt on the bottom of his shoe.

"Well, I'm glad I didn't, and you should be too because this for you," I said, coming up to him, my arms out holding what seemed like something way more important than it was. Like I was delivering some kind of special scroll. The closer I got, the more Stinky Butt perked up. And right when I got to his porch, the puny mutt started growling.

"What's this?" Skunk asked, nodding at me and rubbing his dog's head.

I thought about doing my whole rollout with the

Good afternoon, my name is Lu and whatnot. Just to be funny. Instead I just said, "Camel."

"What?" Skunk took the box.

"A *camel*." I handed him the note from Patty's mom. "Made of fruit." He opened the letter, read it, kissed the air. Then he opened the box. "Don't eat the skin. It comes right off." Skunk was the kind of guy who would try to eat whatever was in front of him. Type of dude that needed to be warned.

He pulled a piece of the "fur" off, pinched off some of the kiwi mash, tasted it. Flashed a distinguished frown. Then looked back up at me. Pinched another piece and gave it to Stinky Butt, who had stopped growling and was now sitting up, waggy-tail, waiting for it. Skunk nodded, then, balancing the camel with one hand—I just *knew* he was about to drop it—got up and opened the front door.

"Ash! Lu out here!" he yelled into the house, all of a sudden.

"Oh, I gotta go." I wasn't expecting him to call for Cotton—Ashley her government name—but I guess he figured I must've been standing there looking silly for a reason. But I wasn't. And if I was standing there looking silly, the reason would've been because he was eating a camel.

"No, you don't," Skunk said, taking a few steps into the house. He was now holding the camel with both hands. Called out for his sister again. "Ash!"

"I'm coming!" she yelled back. A few seconds later Cotton was standing in the doorway, pushing Skunk farther in, away. Stinky Butt followed behind. "Eww, you smell like smoke! And what you eatin'?"

I stood there trying to figure out what to do with my hands. Fold them. Nope. Behind the back. Nope. In the pockets. Maybe. But there was an orange there. A tangerine.

"Hey," Cotton said to me. She had on sweatpants too, and a hoodie, probably because her grandma always kept the air conditioner blasting. I could smell her. Smelled like bacon. Because her grandma was also always frying bacon. Her face, freshly greased.

"Hey."

"What's going on?"

"Chillin'. Had to bring your brother a camel."

"You had to do what?"

"It's Hump Day."

"It's what?"

"My mother."

"Lu, what you talkin' about?"

Without even knowing, I had somehow taken the

tangerine out of my pocket and was peeling it. Just . . . peeling it right there, sliding my thumb under the skin, rolling it back, sliding it off in one piece.

"Nothing." I shook my head. "Forget it." Talk about embarrassing. I split the tangerine and shoved a whole half of it in my mouth so I wouldn't have to say nothing else. Probably was chewing it . . . like a camel. Yikes. Cotton, clearly confused, held her hand out.

What started as just me sharing a piece of stupid delicious fruit turned into a big deal when I got to practice. Because, Patty.

"Well, well, well, look who it is. Lover boy Lu," she announced, standing on the bench as if making some kind of speech.

"What?" I said, giving Ghost and Sunny five.

"Come on, Lu. Don't front. You know I know, and you know the reason I know is because Cotton called me right after you left her house. She told me you showed up to deliver a camel to her brother, whatever that means." Patty hopped down.

"It means exactly what it sounds like it means."

"It does?" Sunny asked, immediately excited about the idea of me showing up to Cotton's house with a huge animal with weird-looking humps growing out its back.

"No. It . . ." I didn't know what to say.

"No, it don't, Sunny. What it means is that he went over there to do some cheesy romantic woo-woo mess with an orange. And Cotton be so up in the clouds about this dude that she fell for it." Patty's eyes rolled to white. "I just want you to admit you like her, goofball."

"I don't."

"You do."

"I really . . . she . . . I've known her forever, just like I've known you."

"You love her."

"Nah, *you* love Sunny."

"What?!" Patty yipped. "Don't try to change the subject, Lu. We talkin' about you. We ain't talkin' about me."

"Whatever. You love him, and he love you."

"That's true," Sunny said, shrugging. "About me loving you. Not about the other part. Don't worry, I don't think you have to love me for me to love you. Because it's like sense, you know? It just exists. Like, um . . . like sky."

"See? Like *sky*, Patty. And you know what? That's what Cotton is to me. She's like sky. Just always been there, to the point that I barely even be noticing her."

"Yo, I swear, Lu, if your skin got darker every time you lied, you'd be midnight by now."

"And still the man."

"But you *not* the man!" Ghost crashed in.

"Neither are you!" I sparked back.

"Sorry, I can't hear you right now. My shoes so loud they making me deaf." Ghost pointed down at his feet, thankfully taking the attention off me. I hadn't even noticed. Looked down, and there they were, new, and bright white, clean. High-tops.

"You got new shoes?" I was shocked. And instantly played back all that mess Aaron brought up yesterday again. "Not because . . . of . . ."

"Man, no. This was my, um, anniversary gift from my mom. She buy me a new pair every year, since it all went down, as a way to say we still a'ight. We good. The old sneakers we always take down to the thrift store because she made up this smart saying that I really believe—one man's trash is another man's treasure." Ghost sat down, started unlacing them.

"Wait. Your mom's the person that made up that saying about the trash and the treasure?" Sunny's eyes bugged.

"Man, no." I shut that down.

"Yes, she did," Ghost insisted.

"No she didn't," I insisted back. "And let me get this straight, you feel like the man just because you got another pair of new sneakers, huh?"

"Pretty much," Ghost confirmed.

"Well, what you get her?" Patty asked, the conversation bouncing between us like a game of hot potato. "What was *her* anniversary gift?"

"I made her tacos," Ghost said, all confident.

"Tacos? Dang. Okay, maybe you the man." I bowed out. I love tacos.

"Yeah, because you ain't make Cotton no tacos. You talkin' about tangerines. *Tuh*." Patty cut her eyes at me. "Okay, Ghost, you really *are* the man." Patty nodded. "But only for today."

"And tomorrow, I'll be the man," Sunny spread his arms wide, like *ta-da*.

After our warm-up laps, I went straight over to Coach, because even though it was Ladder Wednesday, the last of the season, I knew I wouldn't be doing ladders. I'd be doing what I'd been doing. Trying to get comfortable with the hurdles. I had new contacts in, and could see everything clearly, and was ready to get busy.

"Everything cool?" I asked Coach. He had been on

the phone, pacing back and forth, and now was off, but still texting.

"Yeah, yeah. Margo's just a little worried. Tyrone always has a tough time with his allergies this time of year. The wind got the pollen and all that stuff all over the place."

"And the dust," I said, remembering the craziness I went through the day before.

"I should've brought you some goggles or something," Coach said.

"Nah. Too cool for that. The wind ain't as bad today, anyway. Plus, I brought extra contacts, just in case."

"Too cool," Coach said under his breath. "You a trip."

We set the hurdles up—all ten of them—each one a few meters away from the next. Then I took my spot at the finish line, and Coach took his on the sideline, pep-talking. "Ain't nothing to it. Just like we did yesterday. Twelve count, then take the first, and waltz it down the line."

Got it. At least I thought I had it. But when Coach blew the whistle and I started blazing down the track toward that first hurdle, it looked like I was about to have to jump over a goal post. Like I needed one of those sticks to do the pole thingy. You know the . . .

pole thingy event they do in the Olympics? That thing.

And . . . I just couldn't do it. It felt too . . . I don't know. It just felt unjumpable, just like it did on Monday.

"Blew the count?" Coach asked, wondering why I dodged the first one.

"Yeah, sorry," I lied. Then I jogged back up the track to the start. I looked down the lane, staring at the hurdles. *Get up quick. Lead with the knee.*

Coach tapped his head. "Concentrate." I nodded.

Then, *badeep!*

I took off again. *One-two-three-four-five-six-seven . . . eight feet, nine feet, ten feet tall, no no no no no,* and right when I got to the hurdle I jumped it. Like, I just jumped over it—not hurdled, jumped, like hopping a fence.

Coach shook his head, confused. "What's up?"

"I don't know," I said, frustrated. "I just . . . I don't know." I turned my back on Coach and headed back to the start for a third try. All frustrated. The kind of frustrated that stings the back of your throat, waters your eyes. I could hear Coach's steps behind me, following me. When we got back to the start, we looked down the lane at all the hurdles, together.

"What you see today?" Coach asked. Seemed like a

silly question, but that's Coach. Being deep. Like I need Shakespeare to get me over these hurdles.

"What you mean?"

"What. Do. You. See?" He stood behind me, and pointed over my shoulder. I could smell his sweat.

I swallowed. "Um . . . I see hurdles, Coach."

He came back to the side of me. Folded his arms. Nodded. Humphed.

"Take 'em out," he commanded.

"Take . . . what out?"

"Your contacts."

"Wait, *what*?"

Next thing I knew I was back on the track, as the albino Ray Charles.

"What you see now?"

"Coach, I know there are hurdles there. I helped you set 'em up, remember?"

"I know. But can you *see* them? Can you make them out? Or is it like yesterday?"

"It's like yesterday. Everything's a blur." I threw my hands up and let them fall back down, slapping the sides of my legs.

"Good. You know they're there. But you're not focusing on them. Right?"

"Well, I—"

"Right. So twelve to get to the first. Then waltz. Just like yesterday." He stepped to the side. Repeated, "Just like yesterday. On my whistle."

Remember, lead with the knee. Lead with the knee. Come on, come on, come on.

The whistle chirped and . . .

One-two-three-four-five-six-seven-eight-nine-ten-eleven-twelve (knee) *UP!*

One-two-three (knee) *UP!*

One-two-three UP!

One-two-three UP!

And on and on, hurdling until I got to the end of the straightaway. And then Coach blew the whistle. Not like his normal *badeep!* But *badeepadeepadeep-adeeeeeeeeeeep!* And Sunny stopped spinning, and everybody else stopped running their ladders. Even Whit looked surprised.

After he finally stopped, all he said, very quietly, almost whispering, was "Back on the line."

"Back on the line?" That's all I could get out, between breaths.

"Yeah, of course. What you think I was gonna say?" Coach grabbed me by the arm, and started walking me back up the track.

"I don't know. Maybe, 'Good job, Lu. You did it.'"

"Ha!" That's all he said to that. A single laugh.

I ran it again, and again, hurdling the wooden planks, faster and faster, leading with the knee, kicking the air, seeing nothing but what's down the line. Coach was always there to meet me and walk me back, until he wasn't and called out for everyone else to come get me.

"Newbies, come show him some love. The blind boy is hurdling!" And then I watched my friends come from different parts of the track and turn into blurs of random colors, smudges of browns and reds dashing, ghosting around me, gripping my shoulders, slapping me on the back. Honestly, I know it was supposed to be awesome, and it was. But I couldn't see. So it . . . also kinda scared me. It was like I was being haunted! Attacked by funny-acting (and funny-smelling) ghosts, one of them thinking it would be funny to give me a wedgie. Because . . . of course. OF COURSE.

After practice, after I put my contacts back in, after I chased Ghost around for jacking me up like that—I knew it was him—Chris came over to where we were. Where we, the newbies, *always* were.

"Yo, Lu, good job out there," he said, holding his fist out for a pound.

"Thanks, man." I knocked my fist against his, then tilted my head back to put drops in my eyes. "Trying to take one for the team."

"I feel you," Chris replied, as I wiped dripping solution from my cheeks.

"Yo, I been meaning to ask you, how Coach get you to come back?"

"Why you leave in the first place?" Lynn tossed the words in the air as she walked past. Chris sucked his teeth and shook his head.

"Yeah, that's the real question," I said with a shrug. "I mean, Ghost said Coach said it was about grades. But why did you *really* leave?"

"It's not some kind of conspiracy, Lu," Chris chuckled. "My grades *really* slipped. Simple as that."

"*Ah*. So you *really* left because your daddy went upside your head," I joked. Before now, I had only ever seen Chris's father at that first meet—he was now over by the cars talking to Coach, Whit, and Sunny's dad—but it only took one time to see him, to *see* him. Chris's dad was a giant.

"Pretty much," Chris snorted, then added, "And I was failing English, and my pops is a writer. So . . ."

"So he went upside *and* downside your head," Ghost joined in, then jumped into fake-serious mode. "Since he a writer, I got a question. Is 'downside' really a word?"

"He don't know! He was failing English," Patty tagged in. "But I know it's definitely a word. Here's how to use it in a sentence. Ghost is the *downside* of our crew."

"Whatever, Patty, your face is the downside of our crew," Ghost clapped back.

"What?!"

"Nothing."

"Thought so."

"Anyway, Chris, how's the mile coming, man?" I asked, getting to the more important stuff.

"Tougher than I thought, but I'll get there," Chris said, lifting his knees, stretching his legs.

"Better get there quick," Patty said.

"Yeah, man. We only got two days," I reminded him. I also reminded me. "Really, one."

And before Chris could respond, Sunny jumped in.

"Your pace is off." Sunny flipped his discus back and forth from hand to hand.

"What you mean?" Chris asked.

"I mean, your pace is off. You're running nervous. No patience," Sunny explained. He set the discus on the bench.

"I'm running at my usual pace," Chris replied.

But Sunny shook his head and nodded at the same

time, agreeing and disagreeing. "But your usual pace is for the eight hundred," he said. "I can see you from the throwing circle. You're starting too fast, so you'll be rigged by the third lap. Start comfy, settle in on two, dig deep on three, and let it burn on four. It's like running the rings of Saturn." Sunny started making circles in the air with his finger. "The closer the ring is to the planet, the faster it spins. For you, the planet is the finish line." Sunny hopped up, headed back to the track. Waved for Chris to follow. "Let me show you."

Chris looked at us like *we* said it, like we knew what Sunny was talking about. "Saturn?" he chirped.

"Man, just go with it," I replied.

"Wait, Chris." Ghost picked up his bag. "Before you go with it, I got *one* more question about your dad. You think since he a writer, he can write about me?"

"Don't nobody want to write about you!" I snapped.

"No, don't nobody want to write about *you*, blind-o *albindo*," Ghost bucked.

"'Albindo' ain't even a thing. And I might be blind, but *y'all* ain't. Y'all can *clearly* see how fly I am." I pulled my chains from my shirt and thumbed my ears, which is when I realized one of my earrings was missing. "Yo. Where my earring?" My heartbeat skipped. I pinched my left earlobe, started looking around, sliding my feet over the dried-up grass, trying see what on the ground was an old sunflower-seed shell and what wasn't. Now my heartbeat jumped.

"On that note . . ." Patty wrapped her arms around her little sister, who had come to get her. Maddy's braids clicked with red beads. "I . . . gotta go. I can't be out here all night messing with y'all."

But I had to find it. This was a diamond earring my father gave me. It was his first pair, and he gave them to me last year—my first year at Barnaby Middle.

"You think it's on the track?" Ghost asked, peering down at the ground.

"Maybe. Might've fell out when I was running."

So me and Ghost joined Chris and Sunny on the track, and they helped me look up and down the straightaway, but we ain't see it. I even checked along the edge by the grass, but there was no shine, no sparkle between the blades. Finally, the old people were done talking in the parking lot—my mother showed up and had joined the bunch—and they were calling for us.

We headed off the track, back across the field toward the cars.

"Sorry, man," Ghost said, about my earring.

"All good. Maybe I'll find it tomorrow. Not sure how I'm gonna tell my dad, but . . ."

"Hey, at least it's an earring. You can get another earring. Your pops probably got a bunch of those."

"Yeah."

"It would've sucked if you lost something that really couldn't be replaced," Ghost said. "Like how Coach lost his Olympic medal. Now *that's* something to really be messed up about. I mean, I ain't sayin' this don't suck, because it does, but can't nothing be worse than—"

"What you talking about?" I asked.

"Yeah, what *are* you talking about?" Chris followed up, just as confused.

"He's talking about Coach's medal," Sunny confirmed.

"We know that, Sunny. But . . . Coach lost it?" I asked.

"I never told you that story?" Ghost knew he never told me that story. I wouldn't have forgotten a story like that. Ghost glanced around, then said low, "So, when the season first started, I was with Coach. I was having a bad day, and when we were talking about how he grew up in Glass Manor and all that, he told me how his father traded his gold medal for drugs."

"Wow," Chris said, stuck between surprised and sad.

"Yeah, and the worst part is that those were the drugs that—"

"What, y'all wanna sleep out here! What is taking y'all so long?" Coach yelled across the field, cutting Ghost off. "Hurry up!" We all started jogging.

"Wait, Ghost. Ghost," I called out just before reaching the parking lot. He turned to me. "The drugs that . . . what?" I asked, hoping he wasn't going to say what I thought he was gonna say. What I *knew* he was gonna say. I repeated the question. "With Coach's father. Those were the drugs that what?"

And as easy as spitting sunflower-seed shells from his mouth, Ghost spat, "The drugs that killed him."

Those five words made the ride home feel like my skin was a suit I was too big for. Uncomfortable. Tight. Weird. Weirder than the ride home after dropping off the cowboy hat at Mr. Charles's Country Store and bumping into Kelvin. Weirder than running from him when he tried to beat me up, after I had zapped him— the roast and run. Weirder than all the names and the jokes about the way I look. Weirder than everything. Everything. It was like me—the lightning bolt—had been struck by one.

And weirdness makes worry when it comes to moms.

"Everything all right?" Mom asked right on cue as

we turn onto the main strip, past the people ducking in and out of stores, the corner talkers, and bus wait-ers, and kids trying to catch up to parents. She asked if I was all right, when really she already knew I wasn't. She already asked how practice was, and I said *fine*, and *fine* always means *not fine*.

"Yeah." She knew fine meant not fine too.

It ain't like I could just say it. That the drugs sold to Coach's father, his last hit, equals Coach's gold medal in the hands of Goose. My dad. What was I supposed to do? Just ask her if she knew? If she'd seen the medal? If it was tucked away underneath socks and boxers, or in the back of the closet somewhere, maybe hidden in an old pair of sneakers, or laid out with the rest of Dad's jewelry?

"Where's your earring?" my mother asked, now try-ing to change the subject but picking the wrong one to change to. She brushed her hand against my ear while waiting at a red light.

I played it off. Touched my ear. "Huh! I don't know. Guess I lost it."

"Well, your dad's not gonna be happy about that," she said, making me feel *much* better. *So . . . much . . . better.*

"Yeah, well, what he gonna do, take these chains

off my neck?" I said, with a little sting. "Because he can have 'em."

The light turned green. But she ain't move. Just looked at me, until someone behind us honked.

"I'm gonna ask you this one more time, son. And I hope you answer, that way I have a better sense of why you feel like it's okay to give me all this mouth like I've done something to you." Her voice sizzled. "Now, if I have, let me know. But if it's something else, I think—"

"Why you ain't tell me about Dad?" I blurted.

"Tell you what about Dad?"

"About the gold medal? Why y'all got me running on a team, being coached by a man that Dad did dirty?"

"Ah . . ." Mom hesitated a tick. Then, "Okay, now—"

"How can Dad know he messed up somebody like that, and know how to fix it, and not fix it?" I steamrolled. "Ain't that what he always talking about? Fixing his mistakes? Well, one of the biggest ones is right in front of him. So what's the excuse?"

My mother turned right into Barnaby Terrace, turned left onto our street, pulled in front of the house. Parked. Cut the engine. Yanked the key. Sat for a moment.

"Lu." She put her hand on my knee. I turned my head away, hard, looked out the window. Ms. Clark's flower bed had been picked apart, the white rocks sprinkled all around the front of her house, out of place. "Lu, look at me." Nope. Wouldn't look at her. Just felt . . . I don't know. How could Dad just let Coach think his medal was gone forever? How could my mom just be cool with it, and show up and smile in Coach's face every day? How? "Look at me," she repeated, this time cupping my chin and turning it toward her. "You're right. But I need to say this. I knew, and I've been *asking* him, *begging* him to fix it for years."

"Then why won't he?"

She sighed. "It's not my place to tell. But I think you should ask him. Tonight."

"What time he getting home?"

"I don't know."

"I'll wait for him." I opened the door, got out the car. She opened her door and did the same. We walked to the front of the house, and as she pushed her key into the lock, I sat on the step.

"You staying out here?" she asked.

"Yep. Until he gets here."

"What about dinner?"

"Not hungry."

"He might be late, and, even though I know you're

upset, you know I'm not gonna let you sit out here in the dark."

"It ain't dark yet."

Mom let it go. She didn't say nothing else. Just pushed the door open and went inside.

And I sat there. Right there. Like a hydrant with no water. Just looking at the neighborhood, the cars riding by, the noise slowly coming down with the sun. I picked at the cracks in the step, mashing tiny ants with my thumb and swatting at mosquitoes, which for some reason, all of a sudden were interested in me and my blood. I repeated my mantra, pumping myself up, this time to talk to him. *I am the man. The guy. The kid. The one. The only. The Lu.* Over and over again. And in between my chants, I thought about future-new-little-baby sis. How her name couldn't be Gordon. Or Gordy. Or Gordonia. Or Goosey. Or anything like that.

"What you doin'?" a voice came from the sidewalk when I was in the middle of one of my swatting fits. I'd been out there for what felt like forever, but it was probably only like twenty minutes, because time always go slow when you waiting on something. "You look like you conducting the worst orchestra of all time." It was Cotton.

"Hey." I tried to get it together.

"You good?" A funny question. This thing we say to each other all the time, now, all of a sudden, seemed like a for real question. Am I good? Is my family good? My father?

I ain't know how to answer. Just smashed another ant.

"So . . . I'll take that as a no." Cotton walked up, sat down beside me. She was eating a water ice, cherry flavor. "Want some?" She held it out. Again, I ain't know how to answer. "I just got it from down the street, *dang*. I ain't even touch that part yet. Plus it's payback from yesterday. For the orange."

"Tangerine."

"Same thing."

"Pretty much," I said, and if I wasn't so mad about Dad I would've gave Cotton a whole book report on oranges. "But, nah. No thank you," I said. Cotton shrugged. And then we just sat there. She ain't even ask if I wanted to talk about something, and that was nice. We were just chillin', smacking our own legs trying to stop the mosquitoes from eating us alive, watching blue day turn to black night.

And then the streetlights came on. And there was nothing left of her ice but the cup, which she had smashed and folded into a tiny fan. Her mouth was still red. "Yo, I gotta go, before Grandma sends Skunk out looking for me, and I ain't got time to hear his stinky mouth, or Stinky Butt's stinky mouth, with all that yapping." She got up.

"Cool."

Cotton stood in front me, staring, looking for the cracks. "You need a hug or something?" Such a funny thing to ask somebody after you've been sitting with them for a while. Seemed so random, but honestly, I did need a hug.

"You gon' tell Patty?"

"Um . . . of course."

I laughed. Stood up. And hugged Cotton. And it was like hugging cotton. And for a few seconds, I was okay.

A few minutes after she left, my mother opened the door. "Lu, it's getting dark now. He's not here yet, so you need to wait for him inside."

I ain't the type to not listen to my mom. For real. I don't got that in me because my mom, though she cool, can sometimes remind me that she's not playing, and even says to me, *Don't make me remind you how fast cool can turn cold*. I ain't want that. But I wasn't going inside. I wasn't moving until he got home.

I stayed right where I was. Faced forward. Stared at

the street ahead of me when I heard the house door close behind me. And then.

"Scoot over." My mother took Cotton's seat. She was holding an orange, already peeled, already split, and handed me half. "Remember when I named you the Orange Master?"

I peeled a slice from the bunch. Popped it in my mouth. Nodded.

"Remember why?" she asked, and immediately just started laughing. "You thought eating an orange was like eating an apple. Just bit into it. And when you tasted that skin, I thought you were gonna die."

"*I* thought I was gonna die," I said, still mad. But, yeah. Orange skin is gross.

"Yeah." Mom's laugh simmered. "And then I taught you how to peel it. Told you that skin is part of the orange, but not all of it. It's just there to protect all the sweet stuff on the inside."

"And I believed that, until I tasted a grapefruit," I said, this time letting myself laugh a little bit. Just a little bit.

Mom didn't say nothing else. Just put her head on my shoulder. We sat there, just like that, on the front step, eating slice after slice, quiet. And not too much time later—maybe ten minutes—my father pulled up.

He got out of his car, and when he saw us, his face scrunched.

"What y'all doing out here?" he asked, coming toward us.

Mom stood up. "Waiting for you." She leaned over and kissed him on the cheek, he put his hand on her stomach. She put her hand on his chest, almost pressing him to stop. To not come closer. To stay where he was. Then she turned around and went inside.

"Wassup, kid?" he said, cool. Normal. Goose-like. Before answering, I pinched each of my eyes. Peeled my contacts out, held them in a loose fist. Turned him into blur.

"I need to ask you something?" I said, trying to put strong in my voice.

"O . . . kay."

"You said you sold Coach's father his last hit, right?"

"Yeah, and that I'm not proud of—"

"So, you got his gold medal?" If there was ever a time I believed my mother when she called me lightning, if there was ever a moment when I really felt like I could split something in half in a second, it was right then. Those words were a sharp bolt that seemed to come out of nowhere.

I couldn't see him. Couldn't see what his body was

saying, and I ain't really care. I needed to hear what his mouth had to say. I saw the smudge of him move to the left, so I moved to the center of the step to block him from taking Mom's (and Cotton's) seat.

"Okay." He stayed standing. "I . . . there's an explanation."

"How could you take his medal and not give it back to him? It's an *Olympic medal*. There's no way you don't know how important that is to him. That's like . . . I don't know. Maybe the most important thing ever for somebody like Coach. For somebody like *me*."

"I know, but . . ."

"But what? What could you possibly have to say? What could be the reason?"

"I wanted to be him, Lu!" he yelled back. Then took a step back. I couldn't see his face. Didn't want to see it. Glad I couldn't see it. But I could see his arms lifting, probably doing the thing he always did when he was trying to explain something. Rubbing his palms together as if he was washing them. But wasn't no washing this off. "I . . . wanted to be him. Not *be* him, but be *like* him." Dad calmed his voice a little. "He teased me, and he was better than me. A better runner, a better everything. That's why—I wanted you on his team, because he's the best."

"But I thought you said y'all were kids and you ain't take it personal."

"I don't . . . now. But I did back then. I mean, you don't understand. My mother basically took care of him, and then around other people he'd just trash me. Say stuff like:

"You sound like a broken record playing a song that sounds like a scratched CD.

"You sound like a choking Chihuahua.

"You sound like you need an oil change.

"You sound like a breakbeat over broken speakers.

"Make me wanna pop-lock on a cardboard box.

"You sound like a car radio, on scan.

"You sound like a Michael Jackson ad-lib. Not the hee-hee, or the sha-mon.

"The other one.

"You sound like you always about to sneeze, but don't.

"You sound like Donald Duck imitating Daffy Duck trying to imitate Donald Duck.

"You sound like all these things, but you look like a goose.

"Yeah, you look like a goose."

My father's voice was jittery, but not in the way that made me think he was about to cry. It wasn't like that. But I could tell he was feeling it. Made me know it was still stinging.

"Look, I've just been, I don't know . . . I guess . . . too embarrassed to confront him and give it back. He doesn't even know it was me. And the more time that went by, the harder it got."

I heard his feet shuffle, felt him on my side. This time, I scooted over to let him sit.

"Dad, you gotta give it back to him. You always telling me about fixing mistakes. . . ."

"I'm sorry, and you're right. I'm going to give it to him."

"Tomorrow."

"I can't do it tomorrow. I gotta work."

"Tomorrow. Ain't no way I'm gon' be able to keep this secret. Coach too good. Too . . . real. A honest dude. So you gotta do it tomorrow."

My father blew a hard breath, and I could hear the scrapey sound of his fingers scratching his head. I stood up, put my hand behind me to feel for the door. "Oh, and I lost an earring." And quickly added, "Good night."

A NEW NAME FOR PROTECTION:

A Shield . . . that Looks Like
a Heart (Made of Fruit)

The next morning I woke up late. Took a shower, put on a T-shirt, some shorts, and went into the kitchen, and was surprised that Mom was already putting the finishing touches on her masterpiece for the day.

"Morning," I rumbled. "Sorry I slept long."

"Hey, baby." She glanced up from her work. On the table were the guts of a watermelon, a cantaloupe, and one of the green melons. Mom had cut them all up into different pieces, each chunk a different shape, so when put all together they made a big three-color heart. "No big deal. This was an easy one, anyway," she explained. "Didn't need any oranges or even any toothpicks, so I went on and knocked it out without you."

"It's supposed to be a heart, right?" I asked, hoping it was supposed to be a heart. Not sure how I would respond if she told me it was her version of a pair of sneakers, or something like that. I leaned in for a better look.

"Nope, it's a knight's shield," she explained. "Which I guess is kind of the same thing, huh?" Mom looked down at the thing I thought was a heart, then looked back up at me. I knew what she was doing. She was doing that mom thing. The check-in. She was trying to take the temperature of the room, of me, to make sure there wasn't no fever. Make sure everything was cool. But everything wasn't cool. Not yet. Not until the coolest dude I knew fixed the coldest thing he ever did.

If my dad did what he said he was gonna do—which I wasn't so sure about, because I wasn't so sure about anything when it came to him, all of a sudden—then maybe things would start to be okay. But I was going to have to wait and see. And so would he. And, in this moment, so would she. But it was still morning, and she was still my mother, and we still had to go deliver this shield thing that looked like a heart thing to whoever was getting a shield thing made of fruit as a gift, so . . . I just smiled. Held it for three seconds, because if I held it for longer, she'd know I was forcing it, and if I held it for shorter, it ain't really a smile. Hold it for exactly three seconds and my mom stops holding her breath.

I opened the fridge and grabbed the milk and juice. I didn't eat dinner last night and was starving, so I couldn't wait to eat my cereal, which she'd left on the counter for me, as usual.

Mom set her knife on the table and came over to me. Leaned against the counter just like Dad did when he first told me about being named Goose. "Last night your dad got to bed late. He told me what he told you." I chewed on the side of my jaw and questioned if my timing on the smile was off. *Was I a second too long?* I ain't say nothing. Just spooned cereal, but before I could get it to my mouth, she touched my wrist, lowered my hand. "Lu. I know you're disappointed in him. But he's got . . . stuff. That stutter he told you about? Well, that was kinda like him being a lightning bolt. There's not always a known reason why a kid has a stuttering issue, so imagine if you're the one in your class who struggles. Who's teased."

"I ain't gotta imagine that." I was fighting against

my attitude face but could feel my eyebrows dipping into the disrespectful zone.

"I know you don't. Sorry, I know. But think about how you started running and got confident. Well, what if you didn't? What if you weren't as good as you are? Or what if no one was there to tell you you were good? When I met him, your dad was a street dude. At least that's what everybody said. But after I started talking to him, I realized he was more than what people thought about him. He was more than his stutter. More than *Goose*. And that's why we worked."

"I understand all that, Mom. Seriously. But what that got to do with him basically stealing a gold medal?"

She nodded, rested her arms gently on her little belly bump, and sighed. "Nothing. He's wrong. All I'm saying is, he's human too. And sometimes the jokes cut deep. Deeper than we think. And if we don't deal with them, if we don't figure out how to somehow get over them, move past them, we have no idea what they can do to us."

I stayed silent. Just picked my spoon back up and ate.

Today's delivery was way on the other side of town, out by Sunny's house. Actually a little past there, in a neighborhood I never even heard of, probably because it didn't really feel like a neighborhood at all. This area was filled with nothing but steel-and-glass buildings, warehouses, almost no people. It was like the world was over, and the only thing left were parking lots full of navy-blue Camrys.

We listened to Mary J. Blige the whole journey, my mother singing her heart out louder than anyone should ever sing anything, and she only turned it down once we pulled into one of the big, almost-empty lots.

"I think this is the place," she said, checking her paper, then craning her neck to see the number on the building: 300. "You got this, runner?" And as usual, with the shield on my lap, I opened the door. "You're going in there, and down to suite 106. The company is called Sword and Stone."

"Got it."

I got out the car, hit the building's buzzer, and a security guard let me in. I signed my name on the sign-in sheet, which always makes me feel like a grown-up on official business, because it basically means my name means something. Where it says *signature*, I like to just write a squiggly line and pretend it says Lucas Richardson, like everybody else do. "Signature" basically means sloppy name.

"Suite 106, right down the hall." The man behind the desk, who had been, I think, watching a movie on his phone, pointed. When I got down the hall, carrying the plastic case—ribboned and stickered, as usual—and made it to the big metal door marked 106, I knocked. Softly.

No answer.

Knock knock, again. A little harder, trying to balance the plastic case on one hand so that I didn't drop it and have to explain that this was a shield that looks a little like a heart somebody was trying to give you, but the door was locked and I couldn't knock and hold the case at the same time. Thankfully, none of this happened, and instead I could hear somebody coming. Could hear the doorknob jiggling.

The door cracked, and music came blaring out. Rock music. The screamy stuff that makes me want to say *Use your words*, like my mother. A lady dressed in filthy overalls peeked out. There was a big metal mask covering her face, and if it wasn't for her voice, I wouldn't have known if she was a man or woman. She was holding one of those fire-gun things. The ones that make torches. Not what I was expecting in a building with a security guard and a sign-in sheet, but whatever. "May I help you?" she yelled.

"Um . . ." I tried to figure out the best way to begin, over the loud banging and screeching guitars.

"Hold on!" the lady said, noticing that I was holding something. She stepped away from the door, turned the music down, then came back, her mask now flipped up. "Hey. Sorry about that. You the fruit people?"

"Yeah. Uh, good afternoon. My name is Lucas, and I have a package here for—"

"Marina Gonzales. That's me," she said.

"You ordered it?"

"Yep. For myself. Well, for the whole workshop, but mainly for myself." She pulled the door open all the way. "Come on in."

I walked into what seemed like some kind of dungeon, even though it was just suite 106. It smelled like burnt toast. And it looked like Marina Gonzales and the other people who were there—two guys hammering a piece of metal—hated the place. Like they were trying to scrape it up or burn it down.

Marina Gonzales set the big fire-gun down, then took the plastic case from my hands. She set it on a table right by the door, took the cover off, and smiled.

"The shield." She nodded, satisfied. She pinched a piece of fruit from it. *"Nice."*

I looked around. Swords leaned against the wall in the corner. Like, *real* swords. Helmets and big pieces of metal stacked up like giant plates.

"What is this place?" I asked, feeling like I was in some kind of movie. Like dragons were gonna come bust in on us any second.

"This is Sword and Stone," Marina Gonzales said, telling me what I already knew. "We make anything a knight would need."

"A night, like nighttime?"

"No, a *knight*. Like Sir Lancelot."

"Like who?"

"King Arthur?"

"Ah. I know that one."

"So then you understand our name."

"Not really."

Marina laughed. "The story of the sword in the stone. Short version: There was a sword stuck in a stone, and only if you were the destined king could you remove it. Only the person to carry on the tradition of the kingdom would be able to pull the sword from the stone. King Arthur was the guy."

I nodded. "But . . ."

"What do we *do* here, right? Well, we make swords, and helmets, and lances, and all kinds of cool stuff like that. Armor." Marina pointed to the fruit. *"Shields."*

"But . . . why?"

"Um . . . because it's awesome," she said. "I mean, there are all kinds of people who collect this stuff, and a bunch of fairs that use it. Even knight-themed restaurants. But mainly because it's awesome, and . . . tradition."

I nodded again, totally confused, because I ain't never seen nobody just walking around with armor on, or a shield. Like, it would be wild to see Ms. Clark outside holding a sword. Bet wouldn't nobody mess with her limestones then. But that wasn't happening. But I nodded anyway. And all of a sudden, one of the guys who was hammering in the back walked up, pulled a metal spike out his pocket, and stabbed a piece of cantaloupe.

"Hey," he said.

"Hey." Then I looked at Marina Gonzalez with a tight-lipped smile. "I . . . I gotta go."

When I got back outside, my mother had her door open, and at first I thought she was on her way in to get me, which might've led to an even weirder moment, but then I realized she wasn't. Not at all. She was leaning out of the car, puking. It was gross. And on the way home—while I told her about the dragon slayers we'd just dropped a shield off to, and her telling me over and over again that I smell like I've been hanging out inside a barbecue grill—she had to pull over so that she could throw up again. She kept saying she was okay, and that it's just part of having a baby, and that it was way worse with me.

"Thanks."

"Hey, sweetheart, giving birth to lightning don't come easy." She grinned and groaned at the same time.

"Need me to drive?" I asked. Mom's face looked like what brown would look like if brown could be green. But she still started laughing, only because she ain't know there was this one time Dad let me drive. Not far, and only for a little bit. Down the block. So I knew I could get us home if she needed me to.

"No." She swallowed a burp, frowned. "I think . . . I got it."

The rest of the day was pretty much the same thing. Puke fest. When we got back to the house, my mother basically locked herself in the bathroom and . . . yeah . . . it was rough. Worse than what it usually was. She cracked the door for a moment and told me to call Dad and remind him that he really needed to take me to practice. But there was no need to call him, because he walked in the house a few minutes later.

"She okay?" Dad tossed his keys on the table. I was standing in the hallway, listening through the door. Listening to my mom chuck whatever was left in her, out of her, into the toilet. I knotted my face. He came to the bathroom door. Tried to open it, but it was locked.

"Chrissy, you all right?" Now I knew where I got my questioning skills from. Patty's always getting on me about this. It's like, *Dude, you don't hear her in there?*

"No, Gordon. I'm not all right."

"Sorry. I didn't . . . I wasn't thinking."

"Our . . . little girl is giving me the blues today. But I'll be okay. Just make sure Lu gets to practice, please."

"I know, I already planned to take—" Puke sound. *Oof.* Dad turned to me. His face squished up, just like mine. "All day?" he asked me.

"All day," I replied.

"Wow. Okay, go get ready for practice," he said, heading toward the kitchen.

In my room, I went through my usual routine. How I get my head right for battle. First stared in the mirror. White. My hair a yellowish brown. Squeezed the sunscreen out of the bottle and started rubbing it all over

me, still looking, repeating my mantra. *I am the man.*
The guy. The kid. The one. The only. The Lu. Lucky Lu.
Lookie Lu. Lu the Lightning Bolt. I am the man. The guy.
The kid . . . over and over again, rubbing and rubbing
and rubbing, staring at myself. Searching for a crack.

>*You look like a cotton ball dipped in white paint.*

>>*The man.*

>*Like milk. Like somebody supposed to pour you over*
cereal.

>>*The guy.*
>*Like grits with no butter.*

>>*The kid.*
>*Like sugar.*

>>*The Lu. Lucky Lu.*

"Lu, you almost ready?" My dad's voice came
through the door, snapping me out of it. I quickly
slipped on my tight practice jersey. Got my bag, threw
my track shoes in it and an extra pair of contacts. I
grabbed the gold chains off my desk, one by one, slipping them over my head, the metal cold on my neck.
After chain number three, I reached for my earring,
the lonely diamond. I took another look in the mirror,
positioned my fingers to push the pin through my ear
hole, and stopped. Stared at me again.

And it hit me. I always say my mantra as a way to

get gassed up, get me ready to go face whatever. Practice. Races. Kelvins. I always said it's how I get ready for battle, which means, maybe . . . *maybe* it was kinda like *my* version of armor. Not like big and clunky, or a shield that looked like a heart or nothing like that. It wasn't gray and sharp. Maybe for me, my kind of armor was made out of gold and diamonds. Made out of fly. Maybe it was passed down to me by my dad to somehow protect me from what got him. From the wolves. Like, what if I pulled the sword out the stone to carry on the tradition, right? And it came out because I am the man, the guy, the kid, the Lu, Lucky Lu? But what if I don't want the sword? Or the stone? Does that mean I don't get to be King Arthur, and just gotta settle for . . . Arthur? But, *but but but* what if I'm Arthur *the Lightning Bolt*? What he need armor for anyway? He a lightning bolt! Whatever. I'm . . . whatever.

I ain't know what I was really trying to say (to me in the mirror, or to you right now) and I definitely didn't know what them weird people were talking about in that place. Suite 106. And for real for real, I was tripping, but only because for some reason—for some reason—I knew I had to put the diamond back down on the dresser. And, one by one, I took every chain back off.

➤

In the hallway, my father was back at the bathroom door, waiting for my mother to crack it so he could give her a cup of hot tea.

"Ready?" he asked me again.

"Yeah."

"Okay, give me a second."

"Have a good practice, Lu," my mother eeked through the door. Her voice sounded empty. Tired. She grabbed the tea, and my dad jetted down to the end of the hallway, to their room. A few seconds later he came charging back down the hall, stopping at the bathroom again to tell my mother he was taking her car, then meeting me in the living room by the front door.

In his hand was something I'd never seen.

At least not in real life.

Something I'd only dreamed about. A gold medal.

"Here it is," Dad said, handing it to me.

It was heavy. Cold. Gold. In perfect condition. Not a mark or a tear, or a loose thread on the ribbon. Not a scrape or a scratch on the medal. It was—and I don't never use this word—beautiful.

"Took good care of it," I said.

"Yeah," my father replied, opening the door, the

light from outside pouring life into the living room. "But now it's time to put it back where it belongs."

I held it the whole way. I held it like it was mine. Like it was something I could have one day, and I couldn't help but think about what Coach had to go through to get it, and what it must have felt like to have it snatched away. I held it like it was a person. Like it was my little sister. Like it was a heart. My dad and I ain't talk. He just drove. And I just held it. Staring at it. Trying to see myself in that shine.

When we pulled up to the park, pulled into the parking lot, my father killed the engine. And froze.

"Can I get a minute?" he asked, rubbing his hands together.

"Coach right there." I pointed onto the track, where Coach was talking to Chris.

"I know. But I just . . ."

I hesitated. *Ask? Don't ask?* I asked. "You scared to talk to him?"

My father looked at me with eyes I ain't never seen. Eyes that weren't cool. Or slick. Or lovey-dovey like he be looking at my mom. Eyes that said what Ghost's eyes said when he was reading the letter from his dad, or what Patty's eyes said when she told us about that crazy car accident her auntie and little sister were in, or like

Sunny's eyes whenever he talked about his mother passing away.

"*Scared* to talk to him?" he bawked, the same way I did when Coach asked if I was scared to jump the hurdles. "Yes." Straight up. "And . . . and . . . and . . . em-embarrassed." He stuttered. Struggled to get it out. Cleared his throat. Looked at me. I pushed a knot as big as a grapefruit down my throat. As sour, too. And even though I understood where he was coming from, and I felt for him, I put the medal in his hand and got out the car. And before I closed the door, I leaned down and said, "You can fix it."

He nodded.

He sat there for a while. I wasn't sure what he was doing, and honestly I ain't really care. Wasn't none of my business. I had to focus. I had practice. Hurdles to jump. A team to co-captain.

But there wasn't much co-captaining to do because it was Thursday, which meant it was Long Run Thursday, which meant everyone was going to leave the track and go on a run through the neighborhood. I have to admit, it's the worst day of practice for all of us except for the distance runners. Sunny used to run it like it was a warm-up lap—light and easy but way faster than everybody else. Now that he ain't running no more, Lynn always comes in first. And I guess since Chris is back, he'll be right behind her. Me and Ghost came last, usually, but that's okay because we don't run long races. It's stamina work. Coach just wants us to always have another breath. To always have enough leg. To be conditioned to win. Usually Coach hops in his cab and basically chases us through the city, driving just slow enough to see us all, but fast enough to make us feel like he's gonna clip our heels if we start slacking. He would even hit the horn to scare us. But because Coach knew I needed his help with the hurdles, he let the cab stay parked.

"There will be no Motivation Mobile today, which means you all will have to motivate *yourselves*," Coach preached to the team. "I know y'all can do that, because I know y'all want to win. Am I right?"

Everybody nodded.

"Am I *right*?!"

Everybody yeah-yelled.

After stretching, Whit, the leader of the Long Run, took off, everybody falling in line behind her as they all left the track, ran across the field, through the parking lot—past my mom's car, with my dad in it—out of sight.

I didn't go.

Neither did Sunny. He just did what he always did, spun around and flung his discus, letting out strange shrieks. Weird sounds that no human should be able to make. And as Coach set up the hurdles, I took my contacts out. I put them in their case—a pod for each lens—put them back in my bag, and jogged back onto the track.

That's when I heard the car door slam. I looked across the field and there my dad was, walking toward us.

"Who's that?" Coach asked, putting a hand up to his brow to block the sun.

"My dad." I gulped air, thought about what was going to happen. Would Coach yell at him? Would they fight? I couldn't imagine Coach fighting nobody. I couldn't imagine my dad fighting nobody either, but if I had to pick between the two, the Goose is probably taking the turtle. So I hoped that didn't happen. I kept looking, and the closer he got, the more he disappeared. It was like he was becoming walking water.

"Otis," my father called out.

"Goose?" Coach responded. "What's going on?" I couldn't really see, but I knew Coach approached my dad, because I could hear his feet and his voice move toward the fence. And as they got closer to each other, I started walking backward, away from them.

"I need to talk to you for a second," Dad said, as I continued to move backward across the track. They talked, and I walked. They talked and I walked. Backed farther and farther away, their voices becoming quieter and quieter, but their bodies becoming clearer and clearer. Off the track, back and back, onto the field, back and back, a few steps from Sunny. I could see my father holding the medal, the ribbon dangling from his hand. I could see Coach reach for it. Take it. Hold it up so that he could look at it as if it were his baby boy.

"Lu." Sunny tried to get my attention.

"Hold on, Sunny. Hold on." I tried to shush him. Not to be mean, but because I needed to keep watch to make sure these two men ain't start trying to tear each other's heads off.

"Is that your father?"

"Yeah."

"Cool. But Lu," Sunny said again. I turned to see what was up with him, his body nothing but a fog. "You in the way. And if you don't want me to send you to the planet Discobulus with this discus, you should probably move."

"Just give me one more minute, man. Please," I begged, watching Dad and Coach go back and forth. There was a lot of hand moving. A lot of arm waving.

A lot of pointing. Coach put his hand on my father's shoulder. My father wiped his eyes. Then nodded. And then . . .

"Fifty-six, fifty-seven, fifty-eight, fifty-nine . . . one minute," Sunny announced. He didn't even wait for me to move. Just started winding up. I couldn't really see it, but I could tell.

"Okay, okay." I (quickly) got out the way. Started back toward Coach and Dad, who were now sitting on the bench, the same bench me and Sunny and Patty and Ghost sit on every day. Coach was rubbing his face, swiping it with his hand, pinching his nose. Dad was rubbing his hands together. I walked toward them across the grass, already knowing what had happened. What was happening. It was clear, even though the closer I got, the more they faded away.

The rest of practice was Coach blowing his whistle, me running, counting off, jumping hurdles, waltzing, finishing, and my father meeting me to walk me back to the starting line to do it again. On the walks back, Dad would say stuff like, "Getting any easier?"

"No."

"Well, take it from me, it won't. But does that matter?"

"No."

"Exactly. Just remember the upside: you're always going to be bigger than the hurdle."

And then on the last one, the one just before the rest of my teammates came running back across the field toward the track—Lynn in the lead, Chris not far behind—my father, on our way back to the starting line, simply said, "Thank you."

"For what?"

"Remember when I said I can see a lot of me in you?"

"Yeah."

"Well, I think there's some things in you that you see in me, that I didn't even know were there."

I felt the urge to scratch my head to maybe try to wake up my brain. "That's . . . confusing."

"I'm just saying that I'm happy you haven't let the . . . pressure make you small. That you haven't let it eat you."

I just nodded. But it wasn't a good nod. My head felt sudsy like a washing machine. And my stomach felt hot like a dryer. I knew there was stuff that still needed to be cleaned.

By the time I got my contacts back in, everyone else was back, breathing heavy, bent over, pacing back and forth on the track. Coach had the medal tucked in his back pocket—I could see the ribbon peeking out—and was telling everybody to stand up straight. My father was leaning against the fence that circled the track. Fingertips in his pockets. Watching.

"Y'all know my rule. No bending over. Everybody up," Coach commanded. "Whit, who shined out there?"

"I gotta give it to Lynn. She put in work. And also, Chris. He was right behind her, and that's pretty impressive since he hasn't been here all season." Coach gave Lynn and Chris pounds. "But to be honest, everybody pushed through. Patty, Curron, Deja, Brit-Brat, Mikey." Stone-face Mikey smiled. Closed mouth. But still, it was a smile.

"Good, good. That's what I like to hear." Out of nowhere, Coach sat down on the track. Just . . . took a seat. He'd never done that before. "Everybody down. Sit." He patted the track. We all sat, some with our legs crossed, some with our legs stretched out in front of us. Sunny, with his knees tucked.

"This is the last practice of the season. And I need y'all to know, before we go into the championship Saturday, that I'm proud of you. I really am. I know I'm hard on you, but that's because I love you. Sometimes love sounds like . . . get back on the line. Sometimes it's a hard conversation or me blowing the whistle and shaking my head. But as we go into this last meet, no matter what happens, I wanted you all to at least know that. Yes, I want to win. Yes, I want you all to go out there and do your best. But this team has never been about the races." Sunny cleared his throat. "Or the throwing," Coach amended. "This team is about the team. About y'all. About the lane"—Sunny cleared his throat again—"or *circle*, you're in when no one's timing or cheering. The race you're running when no one's looking. Understand?"

A lot of nods.

"That being said, Defenders, let's leave smoke on the track this weekend. Let's leave it all out here. The best never rest."

More nods.

"The best never rest," he repeated.

I looked around at my friends. My new brothers and sisters.

"The best never rest!" This time a little louder.

"The best never rest," Aaron joined in, and I caught the end of it.

"The best never rest." This time me and Aaron said it together.

"The best never rest!" More of us.

"The best never rest!" All of us.

"THE BEST NEVER REST!" And we stood and clapped, and clapped, and clapped.

On the way home, I asked Dad what him and Coach talked about. He said he ain't want to tell me.

"That's between me and Otis," he explained, glancing at me. "But just know we both had some stuff to say. Turns out we both kinda wanted what the other had. But now . . . I think . . . we're good." Dad checked the rearview, then cut his eyes at me, popped me on the arm with the back of his hand. "Hey." I looked at him. "You see how good I treat your mother?"

"Yeah," I said, thinking he was doing the whole change-the-subject thing again.

"Not everybody grew up seeing that," he said, making a right turn. "So you make sure you treat her the same way. And anyone else you love."

Seemed like such a random thing to say, especially since I already knew that. She worries about me all the time. And I worry about her, too. Matter fact, I'd been worried about her all day. Dad and me both had been worried. So we stopped and picked up some flowers on the way home, hoping the smell of them wouldn't make her gag.

When we got inside, Mom was in the living room,

knocked out on the couch. A stream of drool slimed out of her mouth, and my dad bent over and kissed her cheek as if it wasn't there. There was a small trash can beside her—nothing in it, thankfully—and a jar of peanut butter next to the can.

I took the flowers, cut the stems just like she always did, put them in a big plastic Slurpee cup, and set them on the coffee table in front of her.

"What we gon' eat?" I asked my dad softly so I didn't wake my mother. Dad shrugged. Opened the fridge.

"Any peanut butter left?" he asked. I crept over and grabbed the jar that was on the floor.

"Yeah."

"Well, let's see what we can do."

We called it the Newbie. It was bread. Peanut butter. Honey. Bananas. Middle bread. Grape jelly. Grapes (cut in half so they look like purple bumps). Mashed-up kiwi that we called fruit guacamole. Top bread. Finished off with an orange slice (of course) with a toothpick through it.

And it was delicious.

9

A NEW NAME FOR ME: Me (Maybe)

The next morning, when I came into the kitchen, my mother was sitting at the table. The flowers me and Dad got for her she had moved to the kitchen, in front of the window, where they belonged. But they were still in the Slurpee cup. She was flipping through one of her art magazines.

"Good morning, Lu." She glanced up.

"Morning," I replied, yanking the fridge open, reaching for the milk and orange juice. "Feeling better?"

"At the moment," she said, rubbing her stomach. "Baby girl's not gonna put up with no mess, that's for sure."

I poured my cereal, juice, the usual. Then sat down at the table. "What you doing?"

"Looking for inspiration," she said. She closed the magazine. Looked at me. "No deliveries today." A day off. *Yes.* "But your father wants you to hang with him. That man—he works like he's trying to win first place at it." Apparently, no days off for me.

"He's here?" I only asked because usually when I wake up, Dad be already gone. He got home late most nights, and left early most mornings, running around doing whatever he does to help people struggling with addiction stuff.

"Yeah, he's outside cleaning out his car."

What my mother meant by cleaning out his car was making sure it was spotless. My father drove an old car. A really old car. So old that it seemed new. So old that it felt like a spaceship from the future. By the time I got out there, he was spraying shiny stuff on the tires to make sure the black wasn't just black, but shiny black. A black that seemed to glow and sparkle when the sun hit it.

"Wassup, man," he said, looking over his shoulder. He was squatting and spraying. Squatting and spraying.

"Hey." I looked down the block. Up the block. No

one outside yet. "Mom said you want me to hang with you."

Dad put the spray can down. Stood up. "Don't do me no favors." He smirked.

"I ain't mean it like that."

"I know," he said. "I want to give your mom a day to chill out. Hopefully she won't be too sick and she can really kick back and enjoy herself without you stinking up the joint. Plus, you've never seen what I do. And after yesterday . . . today might be a good day to check it out."

An hour later we were cruising. My father's a little different from my mother because he plays my music— good music—all the time. And he plays it loud. Like he young. Like he Skunk.

We rode through Barnaby Terrace, passing Cotton's house—I couldn't help but look to see if she was outside—Patty's old house, where her mother still lives, the grocery stores, the owners of those grocery stores hosing down the sidewalk, the churches—Dad turned the music down whenever we passed one—dollar stores, general stores, which are basically five-dollar stores, more dollar stores, a ninety-nine-cent store, Everything Sports, which was my favorite store, and eventually we turned into Glass Manor and pulled up to the basketball court. It was busy. Lots of people already playing, running back and forth, shirts and skins, screaming and calling for the ball. Girls. Women looking on. Looking at their boyfriends, I guess. Or maybe not. Maybe some of them were waiting to play. And people who were messed up. People leaning, and scratching. People too awake, and too asleep.

Right after we got out the car, another car pulled up.

"Listen," Dad said, locking the doors. "I know everybody here. So you're fine. But if I call your name, I need you to come immediately. Got me?"

"Yeah." I glanced at the car parked behind us. The person opened the door, rose up from the driver's side.

"Yo." A familiar voice came over my shoulder.

"There she is," my dad announced. "The great Whitney Cunningham."

"Whit?" Whit walked over, gave my father a hug. Gave me a playful smush to the face. "What you doing here?" I asked, confused.

"What *you* doing here?" she asked back, just as confused.

"I'm here because he"—I jerked a thumb at my father—"brought me. Plus we giving my mother a day off."

Whit laughed. "I know. I'm just joking. Me and

Goose talked about it yesterday. I knew you were coming." She turned to my dad. "You tell him why we here?"

"Not yet. Figured you should tell him," Dad replied.

"Well, Coach told me you met my brother," Whit explained.

"The Wolf?"

"Yeah." Whit did a half eye-roll. "Torrie. Well, your father has been trying to help me . . . help him. Help me help him. We've tried a few times already, just with the letters. I've written several. But Torrie won't bite. They haven't been enough. So today, I decided to take off work and come down here myself and read it to him out loud."

"Here?" I darted my eyes to the court, a busy mash-up of sound and body.

"Here," Whit confirmed.

"That's why I had to get permission for you to come, kid," Dad explained. "This is a big deal. And it's personal."

"It's life," Whit said, sort of shrugging. "And it's never a bad time to witness life."

But I felt funny about it. Funny in a queasy way, like I wasn't supposed to see whatever I was going to see. Kind of how I felt when Dad was talking to Coach. And the funny feeling got worse when we actually got over to the court, and everybody shouted my father out.

"Goose!" a big dude built like a tank boomed.

"Whaddup, Goose." From a dude my dad called Sicko. He was kneeling on the sideline, scratching a muscular pit bull behind the ear. My father whispered to me not to touch it.

"Goose, don't come in here making no trouble," a young dude, dribbling the ball back and forth between his legs, warned.

"I was making trouble when I was your age, Pop. You know I ain't on that no more," Dad replied. Then he turned to one of the other guys. Tall, cut-up dude, looked like he was supposed to be on somebody's NBA team. "You good, Big James?"

The guy called Big James nodded. "Better than everybody else on this court. It's lunchtime, and these fools ain't nothing but food." He rubbed his fingers together. "Bread and cheese."

"Yeah, whatever," Pop said.

"You out your mind."

"I just took *your* money, James!"

"Yeah, because Sicko a bum."

"Keep talking, James, and this here dog'll show you who's food."

My father laughed before finally introducing me and Whit to the crew.

"Everybody, this is Whitney. Wolf's sister." Dad followed up with a quick warning. "No slick talk. I'm not playing."

"Ain't nobody gon' say nothing slick," Pop said . . . slick.

One guy whose name I didn't know mumbled too loud to be a mumble. "Uh-oh. I already know what this about."

"And this is my son, Lu," Dad announced.

I almost waved, but waves be weird. So I nodded. Chin up.

"Wassup, li'l man," it seemed like everybody said.

"Wassup."

"You play?"

"No," my father said, before I could even try to say it myself. Then Dad leaned into me. "Go sit over there." He pointed to a bench in the corner. And . . . and . . . sitting on that bench was . . .

No.

No no no.

Not again.

Kelvin Jefferson.

Just sitting there.

jason reynolds

Kelvin Jefferson.

Watching the games.

Kelvin Jefferson.

Eating sunflower seeds.

Right when I noticed him, he noticed me. And right when he noticed me, I swallowed what felt like a basketball.

"Over by that kid." My father nudged me. "Shouldn't be no longer than ten minutes."

On the walk over, I prepared myself. *Play it cool. Play it big. Head up. Chin up. Get ready to fire back on whatever this dude says.*

Yo, Kelvin, you smell like your blood ain't blood. It's trash juice pumping through your veins.

Like bubble gum chewed too long.

Like a fart's fart.

Like your whole body is a underarm.

Like your underarms are upper-body booties.

Like bad milk.

Like good milk. (Milk is weird.)

Like last week, this week.

Like boiled vegetables.

Like something wrong with you.

Like something wrong with you.

Like something wrong.
SMELLLLLLVIN!

I was ready. And just in case after I said all this, things went left, I thought about Coach's hurdling advice. My forever plan B. *Get up quick. Lead with the knee.*

But when I got to the bench, Kelvin just glanced at me. Scooted over.

"Wassup," he said, shaking seeds from the bag into his hand.

"Wassup," I said, sitting, but still locked and loaded. Still ready. Waiting for him to do what he always did.

But it never came. He just threw the fistful of seeds into his mouth and crunched on them. Like, just chewed them all up like they ain't have no shells. Chewed and crunched like he was mad at them. Then dropped his head and spit the chewed seeds and shells out. Just chewed and spat, shards of sunflower seeds flying all over the place, all over the ground between his feet. And when I saw the mess he'd made, I also noticed his shoes.

High-tops. With the high part cut off, to make low-tops. I knew those shoes. I knew who made them that way. Ghost. Those were Ghost's sneakers. At least they used to be. Now they were . . . Kelvin's?

I had had so much I wanted to say to him. So many questions. But in that moment, right when I looked at his bashed-up shoes, he caught me looking, and I snapped my head up and forward to see whatever was happening on the basketball court.

You saw nothing. And he ain't see you see nothing. Nothing at all.

I made a tight fist, just in case. Then I felt a tap on my arm. "Want some?" Kelvin held the bag of seeds out. No blue-and-purple spots on his arm. No marks.

I nodded, rolled my fingers back. Opened my hand.

We were quiet for a while, watching the court, the men talking trash like they hated each other even though I knew they didn't, some of the girls watching and cheering, others on their phones, the leaners and scratchers . . . the Wolf. Eventually, after I got tired of Kelvin spitting all over the place, I tried to teach him how to open a sunflower seed like a pro. The way Ghost taught me. How to be patient, calm. How to move it around, how to stand it up, how to crack it open. But he wasn't getting it.

The whole time all this was happening, Dad was on the other side of the court with Whit and the Wolf. The Wolf just kept shaking his head, and Whit had her hands pressed together like she was praying, but she wasn't. She was begging. My father had one hand on Whit's shoulder, and one hand on her brother's shoulder, almost like he was stopping either of them—maybe both of them—from running.

And then the game ended. And the losers handed over wads of cash. And my father walked out onto the court.

"Listen up!" Dad yelled out. Everybody looked up, and honestly, even though I've always seen my dad as cool, I was surprised he got so much respect. "Whit has something she wants to say to Torrie. And she wants y'all to be witnesses."

The guys sort of mumbled and grumbled, some shook their heads. Folded money and tucked it in their socks, making their ankles look swollen. Some sat on the ground. Unlaced their sneakers. Others sat on benches next to the girls.

Whit came to the middle of the court. She looked shaky and shy, which I wasn't used to. My father stood next to her. She pulled out a piece of paper, unfolded it, and began to read it. Loudly.

"Torrie, when we were kids, you were the best big brother a little sister could ever ask for. You taught me how to walk. And eventually, you taught me how to run. You taught me how to be strong, and how to push it to the limit, and you were one of the funniest people I've ever known. That's where that stupid howl came from. You chasing me around the house, telling me the tickle monster was coming, howling like a fool. And then something happened. Something changed. I know that who you are today is not you. It's the drug. And I'm not judging you. I've never judged you. Because we all have something we're dealing with. We all have some kind of addiction eating at us. For some, it's jealousy. For some, it's the fear of not being accepted. For some, it's the feeling of being overwhelmed. For some, it's the pain of being different. We all have a mountain to climb. But, Brother, it's time for your mountain to be moved." She paused. Sniffled, and wiped tears from her cheeks. Now everyone was looking, listening. "But . . . I can't move it. I've tried. Goose has tried. We can't move it, but you can. You can do this. You need to do this. I need you. Our parents need you. These beautiful kids I coach, *because* of you, need you. You need you. So . . . please . . ." She looked up at her brother, who was standing there, skinny and weak and wet. "Please."

She folded the letter and put it back in her pocket. I glanced over at Kelvin, and he was wiping tears from his face too, but trying to do it in a slick way so I wouldn't catch him. Turned away from me as if there was something interesting to look at out on the street.

My father glanced around at the court and nodded, and all of a sudden, these tough guys, Pop, and Sicko, and Big James, and everybody else just started up.

"Yeah, Wolf. It's time."

"It's time, man."

"Mess gon' kill you, dude."

"Yeah, get some help. Ain't nothing wrong with that."

"All I know is, that's your sister. Your sister, man."

Sister. I don't know if the word "sister" hit a switch in my brain or what, but all of a sudden I start thinking about my future-new-little-baby sister. The second bolt of lightning. But not lightning at all. Snowflake. The snowflake that hopefully would never have to know what it means to disappear. I wanted to be a real big brother. A *big* big brother. And not just when she was little, not just when I was teaching her how to do cool stuff like beat all the boys on the track, or how to roast when she needed to, but when we got old, too. Gotta finish strong. All the way through. Gotta be a big brother like . . . well, like how Patty a big sister to Maddy. Gotta really look out. Look after her the same way all these people were trying to look out for and look after Whit's brother.

Everybody joined in, and soon, the Wolf—Mr. Torrie—walked to half-court, where my dad and Whit stood. And smiled.

And people started clapping. And clapping. And Kelvin faced forward again and clapped too. He let the tears come. Looked at me, face all wet, and was different. Like his skin had been peeled back, and whatever was underneath was what connected him, somehow, to what we were all watching.

I put my hand out. He gave me a five. And I left.

Me and Dad followed Whit and her brother to the rehab center. My father said he always liked to go with them just to make sure everything went smooth.

"You never know, man," he said, scratching his forehead. "I've seen a lot of wild things happen." But nothing wild happened this time. We pulled up to the center. Whit and Torrie got out.

"This is the boring part," Dad said. "But we gotta do it. There's nothing to see, and nothing to do." He reached in the backseat and handed me some pamphlets. "Might as well read."

"But it's summertime," I said, opening the passenger door.

"What that mean? Your brain don't work no more?" Dad joked, closing his.

I sat in the waiting room for what seemed like forever, reading these papers about detox, and how sometimes before they can even start real treatment they have to let the drugs pass through people's bodies, and how terrible it feels to, like, get all the stuff out of you. I also read about the twelve steps people sometimes use to get clean. It said 12 STEPS MADE SIMPLE, which made me wonder what the twelve steps made difficult were. Anyway, the simple ones in the pamphlet were:

1. Honesty
2. Hope
3. Faith
4. Courage
5. Integrity
6. Willingness
7. Humility
8. Discipline and Action
9. Forgiveness
10. Acceptance
11. Knowledge and Awareness
12. Service and Gratitude

I understood most of these, but the one that kept tripping me up was number five. Integrity. I just couldn't figure it out. I mean, I know what most of the others are, and some of the other ones I wasn't completely sure about, I could kinda guess. But "integrity." That ain't even made up of no other words accept for "in" and "grit," but that don't make no sense.

"Dad." I nudged him. He was sitting right next to me, making sure Whit and Mr. Torrie knew what they were doing, even though there was a counselor person talking to them too. He didn't answer, so I nudged him again. "Dad."

"Yeah?" He turned toward me.

"What's integrity?"

"Huh?"

"What's integrity?" I repeated.

"It's like, um, how do I explain it?" Now he turned his whole body to face me. "It's like the good parts of you, that . . ." He stopped, tried to gather his thoughts. "You know that gold medal I just gave back to Otis?"

"Yeah."

"See how the gold didn't change? Didn't turn any other color?"

"Yeah."

"See how it was still heavy after all those years, and

how it didn't bend or start to disintegrate?"

"Yep."

"Well, think of integrity as the gold medal . . . inside you."

When we finally made it home, it was evening and the sun had just started to come down. The block was buzzing as usual, and inside our house was as well. My mother was up and listening to her old music, the sound of it, and the smell of something delicious, smacking us in the face at the door.

"Hello!" my father called out.

"Hey!" Mom called back. She was in the kitchen, two-stepping and holding a carrot like it was a microphone. "Y'all had a good day?" she asked, before leaning over and giving me a kiss. Then doing the same to Dad.

"Yeah, pretty good," he said.

"Good. What about you, Lu? Learn anything?" she asked, because she's a mom and that's all they really be caring about. They just want you to learn stuff all the time.

"Actually, I did." I flashed a fish face like, *so . . . boom.*

"Oh yeah? Wanna talk about it?" she asked, and

before I could answer, my father jumped in and hugged her, and started slow dancing with her, stepping and spinning her slowly between the table and the counter. I can't front. He was smooth with it. Not just the dancing, but with the interruption. He knew this one was for us.

"*Ahhh.* Now I get it. *This* is why you let him get away with calling you a Pepperoni on your first date," I joked.

"Pepperoni?!" he yelped, pulling away.

After I washed up, it was time for dinner.

"On the menu tonight," my mother started, "steamed carrots, mashed potatoes—both of which I got from the farmers' market today—"

"You went to the market?" I asked, only because we usually only go once a week.

"Listen, I got to spend the day how I wanted to spend it. So I went and saw my girl Frankie." Mom was about to continue but instead just shut me down with, "Mind your business." She smiled. "Anyway, we having fresh organic carrots, fresh organic potatoes, and"—she opened the oven—"Salisbury steak!"

"Let me guess, you went all the way to Salisbury to get it?" my father joked.

"What's Salisbury?" I asked. I had Salisbury steak before but never asked that.

"A city," my mother replied.

"Where?"

"Maryland," from my dad, who, as usual, was tucking his chains in his shirt.

And at the same time my mom answered, "Europe."

So it sounded like *Murope*.

"Don't matter. I ain't go nowhere but to the back of the freezer for these."

Honestly, it didn't matter where she got them from. They were delicious, even though I felt like they were supposed to be on hamburger buns. Kinda reminded me of a sloppy joe, before it was turned into sloppiness. An unsloppy joe. With steak sauce.

Halfway through the meal, after I told my dad the whole story about the people from Sword and Stone, and imitated the dude with the spike, my mother took her knife and started knocking it against her cup. Which, after that crazy story, seemed pretty normal.

Clunk clunk clunk clunk clunk.

"Doesn't really work the same with plastic," she said, setting her knife down. "Anyway, I would like to make a toast." Mom put on her best fancy voice. It was probably the voice she thought Mr. Charles Ringwald was supposed to have, but definitely didn't. I thought about Sunny and his grass-and-dirt toast, and figured maybe me and Mom and Dad could do that too at some point. Maybe after the baby was born. "To Lu, for finishing another amazing season on the track. It doesn't matter what happens tomorrow. I'm so proud of you."

"I'll toast to that," my dad added.

"And little sis is proud too," Mom tacked onto the end. We lifted our glasses. Juice for Mom. Beer for Dad. Milk for me.

"Cheers."

"Cheers!"

"Boomticky tacky cheers!" I blurted.

"*What?*" My dad twisted his mouth, but my mother, she liked it.

"Nothing, just . . . Sunny."

Sip.

"About your little sister. You come up with a name yet? Any ideas?" Dad asked, as we all set our cups down.

I pushed my plate to the side, propped my elbows up on the table, and put my hands together, but with only the fingertips touching. I glanced at my mother, thinking she was going to give me knife eyes. But she didn't.

"Well, it's been weird to try to figure out what to

name her. My newest good name ideas are Valencia, or Mandarin, or Clementine, but when I really started thinking about it, thinking about what she is to us, to me, I realized that there's only one thing she could be called."

"And what's that?" My mother tapped her fork to her lips, sideways'd her head.

"Lightning."

Mom's eyes got big, and she looked at my father. He lowered his chin.

"Lightning," she repeated, then repeated again. "Lightning. Gordon, you . . . uh . . . wanna say anything?"

Dad still didn't look up. Just shook his head.

"Gordon!"

Now he looked up. "Um. Okay, what do you think about Lightning for a middle name?"

"Middle name?" I asked, not knowing where this was going.

"Yeah," Mom agreed, quick-fast. "And for her first name we go with something simple. I've always liked Christina, after me, or Melanie. Or even Erin. I love Erin for a girl."

"But you said I could name her. You told me that was my job, so . . ."

"I know, but—"

"So, I choose Lightning." I shrugged, took another swig of my milk, swallowed. "And for short, I'm going to call her Light."

My mother's eyes got big again. But my father didn't drop his head this time. He smiled.

"Light." He nodded. Smiled a little bigger.

"I think I like that. Lu and Light." Dad started slow-nodding. I looked at Mom, and those lightbulbs in her cheeks came on.

"But it's really Lightning," I reminded them. Just to be clear.

"Okay. But can we come to a compromise? Light is good. Come on, man, I'm puking every day to get her here. Work with me."

She had a point. "Okay, Light it is."

Light it was.

After dinner, I took a shower to wash the day off. The car and the court. Kelvin and the sneakers. Whit and the Wolf. Rehab and detox. Twelve Steps and gold medal. So much. So many things on me. In me. And now, I had Light. Light to look for. To look after. To keep on. I went into my room, took out my contacts, blurred out, laid in my bed, and thought about her. Light. My sister.

10

A NEW NAME FOR DEFENDER: Family

Race day. Not just any race day. Championship day. I went to bed early, so I woke up early. Earlier than everybody else. I took a shower, put my sunscreen on, laid out my Defenders uniform. The electric blue and gold. The muscle arm, with the hand squeezing the wing. The bold lettering: DEFENDERS across the front.

"One more time," I said to myself.

I got dressed, went out to the kitchen to put the coffee on for my mom and dad. I'd seen my mother make it every day for basically my whole life, so it was no big deal. And I knew they'd want it. They always wanted it in the morning. Plus the smell of it, I knew, would wake them up. The smell of that stuff would get any-body up. I poured myself some orange juice. Poured myself a bowl of cereal. Drank. Ate. Then opened the fridge again to grab a few oranges. I chopped them into slices, then put them in one of my mother's many Tupperware containers like I always did every week, for every meet, mainly for me, but also to share with my teammates.

Then I sat at the table, folded my arms, and waited.

Five minutes went by. Nothing.

Ten. Nothing.

Fifteen. I couldn't take it no more, so I went and knocked on their door.

"Guys?" I said soft. I knocked again.

"Lu, we're up. We're up," my father groaned through the door. Then I heard him mumble some-thing, and my mother tell him to chill out because it's championship day. And that meant I was excited.

Not really excited. More like nervous. Or both. Excited and nervous. Excited to smoke everybody in the hundred, but still nervous about those hurdles. I knew I could do it. I knew what it took to do it. I had it down to a science. To a count. *One-two-three-four-five-six-seven-eight-nine-ten-eleven-twelve*. **Up**. Then, *one-two-three **up**, one-two-three **up***. I went to sleep counting and woke up counting and counted the orange slices, the number of gulps in the glass of juice, the spoonfuls in a bowl of cereal. I knew it. I knew I knew it. But I was still . . . nervous.

"Guys, I want to get there kinda early," I spoke back through the door. "You know, just to warm up, and make sure I'm ready."

My dad grumbled again. But my mother answered, "Okay, baby. Okay, okay. We're getting up."

When they finally made it to the kitchen, coffee was ready. Half cup for Mom, and I left the cereal out for them.

"How you feeling, runner?" my mother asked.

"I'm okay. Just jumpy."

"I bet," my father said, spooning soggy flakes into his mouth. "I would be too."

"But you're gonna do great. Because you are great. You were born great," my mom tossed out what seemed like some of her own mantra.

"Okay, okay." My dad stopped her. "You're putting it on a little thick."

"But he is," she said, not even caring what Dad was talking about.

"I know, but he's a little stressed out," Dad said, trying to get her to understand.

"He's my son, and he's great." Point-blank, period. No reason to argue. But Dad tried anyway.

"He's my son too, and I know he's great, but maybe . . . maybe he just wants a little time to get himself together without the pep talk before the pep talk." Dad shrugged. "That's all I'm saying."

"I'm good," I said, stopping them from going down this long road. They were nervous too. They always were when it came to me running, but instead of just admitting it, they did this every week. And my father had only been to one meet this year. The first one. Yes, that's a little bit because of work, but also because he can't take the stress of seeing me run. Because he ran. And he knows what it's like. "Seriously, I'm good," I repeated. "But I just need to get to the park."

Before we left, I went back to my room and looked at all the jewelry on my dresser, the necklaces laid out like a gold river. My armor. The one diamond earring. None of it really meaning what it meant to me before finding out all the stuff about my dad and the medal. It all meant something else now. I glanced from the gold on the dresser to the me in the mirror. Mantra.

I am

The man.

The guy.

The kid.

The one.

The only.

The Lu.

Lucky Lu.

Lookie Lu.

Lu the Lightning Bolt.

Then I grabbed one chain—just one—and put it around my neck. I mean, they were my father's. And I'm his son. Gold. Shining. Cool.

In the car, my mother—I repeat—my *mother* played my music—I repeat—*my* music. And my dad, who was driving my mom's car, turned the radio up, like he always did. Loud. We rolled the windows down. It was another breezy summer day, more weird weather, which, honestly, was nice for a championship meet, because people wouldn't mind sitting outside in the heat for hours, but tough sometimes because it's hard to run against the wind. If the wind was to your back, it would push you forward. But if it was to your front, it would slow you down. And don't even get me started about what happens if it pushes Sunny's discus, like Coach was saying. Mess around and take somebody out.

It was still kind of early when we pulled up to the park. There were a few people there, but it wasn't jumping yet. Just the early birds. The other runners like me, who needed a little extra time on the track to warm up.

The only person from my team who was there already was Chris. I wasn't surprised. If I was gone the whole season but then had to run a mile in the championship, I'd be nervous too. I'd be just as nervous as I already was, because we both had to kill it in order for our team to win.

When I got to the track, Chris was folded in half, touching his toes, coming back up, then touching his toes again, and coming back up again.

"Hey, man," I spoke.

"Wassup, Lu," he replied.

"Nervous too?" I asked, slapping his hand.

"Super nervous."

We stretched a little. Not a whole team stretch, but just enough to wake the legs up. Then we decided that the one thing both of us could do to get in the zone was some high knees. I would need them to get over the hurdles, and Chris would need them on that tough final stretch as he was running the rings of Saturn. So we high-kneed around the track, starting slow, then speeding up after every hundred meters.

By the time me and Chris finished the lap, people had started trickling in. Curron, Brit-Brat. Then Mikey, Freddie, Deja, Krystal, J.J., Melissa, Aaron. Then Ghost. With his mom, and his aunt, and his cousin. Oh, and Mr. Charles Ringwald was with them too. They all held signs. And Sunny, with his father, and his teacher with the wild hair and tattoos. And Patty, with a million people, including her mom, her uncle, her little sister, shiny-faced Cotton, Skunk, and even Stinky Butt. Her aunt wasn't there, though.

After a whole bunch of wassups, me, Sunny, Patty, and Ghost sat on the bench, going through the motions of changing shoes and talking trash. Patty was drawing a star on Sunny's forearm, and Sunny was going on and on about Patty's nails, which were the goldest gold I'd ever seen. Ghost was telling Patty that he still wanted to hear her freestyle, and Patty was telling Ghost that she'd do it, as soon as he made her tacos. Sunny said he thought freestyles were supposed to be free, and I just sat there staring at the track. Zoned.

"Yo, you good?" Ghost asked, tapping me on the arm. He had just changed his shoes, swapping out his new bright whites for his silver bullets.

"Yeah. I think so." But I wasn't. Almost, but not yet. "Yo, I need to say something to you."

"Wassup?"

"My bad about what I said when we first met. About your shoes."

"What? Man, that was a long time ago. And it was a joke," Ghost said, zipping his duffel bag. "You let Aaron get in your head."

"I know, but still. I just felt . . . like, who is this dude thinking he can just come and try to outshine me?" I glanced at him, then back to the track. "I don't know, man. But it wasn't cool. So I just needed to say that. Before we got old." I put my fist out.

"Old? First of all, I ain't never getting old. So, yeah. And second of all, my albino homeboy, get ready to be mad *again*." He bumped his fist with mine. "Because I'm winning that hundred-meter dash today."

We joked about that—because I was *definitely* taking first—while my mother bopped around, offering everyone orange slices. When Whit showed up, she talked to my dad for a bit, as everybody else changed shoes and hit the track, along with other teams that were pulling up left and right, the park going from rattle to rumble. Watched the stands fill with hyped-up family members wearing shirts to match whatever team they were rooting for.

This was my tenth track meet as a Defender, and

by now, it had become routine. We had our own kinda rhythm. Everyone knew what to expect from everybody else. What was what and who was where.

And like I said, Whit was there. But Coach wasn't. So something was offbeat.

"Let's focus, everybody. Stretch it out. You know what to do," Whit said, in Coach's style.

"Where Coach?" Deja asked.

"I'm about to call him now," Whit said. "But you don't need to worry about where Coach is. You're here, so you stretch. Keep your mind on the meet." She tapped the side of her head, then stepped away to make the call.

"A'ight, Defenders, let's get to it. Squats. And, down!" Aaron started, and I followed. I wasn't in the mood to argue or try to do anything to mess with him. It was championship day, and on championship day, more than any other day of this season, we had to be together. We had to be a team. And since Aaron's the captain—the first captain—I just listened. Squatted. Counted. ". . . four, five, six . . ." I glanced over at Whit. Watched her hang up. Start texting. Call again. "Lunge with the right. And . . . down! One, two . . ." She left a message. At least I thought she did. Had her back to us, so I couldn't tell what she was saying. Hung up.

". . . eight, nine, ten. And to the left. Down!" Whit started walking back over to us. Stopped. Checked her phone. It was ringing. "Back to the right. And, down!" Her face. It changed. That look. One I had seen in all of us. In me. Something—"five, six"—was—"eight, nine"— wrong.

"And back to the left!" Aaron called out. But I stood up. Didn't lunge. He counted but I just stood there. "Lu! Down!" he commanded. But, no. "What's wrong with you?" he asked. Patty glanced behind her. Caught Whit's face. Stopped stretching too. A few seconds later no one was counting, and we all were standing straight.

"What is it?" I asked Whit. She walked right in the middle of the circle.

"Something's happened."

"To Coach?" My mind just jumped there. Instinct.

"No." Whit patted down the air. "No, no, no. Coach is okay. But . . ." Whit looked up, then looked back at us. "His son."

"Tyrone?" I took a step forward.

"He had an asthma attack. A bad one. Allergies. So Coach is at the hospital. He . . . doesn't think he's gonna make it."

"Tyrone ain't gon' make it?" Ghost's voice cracked. Patty grasped Sunny's arm.

"I don't know about Tyrone. But I'm saying Coach might not make it . . . here."

"To the meet?" I asked.

Whit nodded. "We're gonna have to win it without him."

I could almost feel the team deflate. It was like normally Coach was the air and we were the balloon, but now Coach was the needle that popped us. "Get back to your stretches. I'm gonna go check the paperwork and make sure we have everything in order. We're gonna win this thing. The best never rest!"

"The best never rest," a few of us replied, but not all of us, and definitely not all rowdy, all pumped up like we should've been.

As Aaron continued to call out the stretches, I did them, but I just didn't feel it. Something about doing this without Coach . . . it didn't seem right. It just didn't. And even though I ain't know all the details— couldn't see Tyrone trying to breathe, or Coach trying to save him—I didn't need to, to know something was in the way. Something was *not* right. So finally, I stood up again.

"What now, Lu?" Aaron asked.

"I ain't doing this."

"What?" Aaron popped up. Not just him. Him and

a bunch of other people, including Curron and Mikey.

"I'm not doing it without him," I repeated. "And for real for real, I don't know how y'all could."

"Dude, this is what Coach would *want*," Curron said.

"How you know?"

"Because this is what he trained us for. You think all this was so that we *don't* run?" Aaron followed.

"Yeah, what you think 'the best never rest' means?" Mikey piled on.

"I don't care what it means. Right now, Coach is at the hospital with a baby that can't breathe, and you want to be out here running?"

"Yeah, but how you know this ain't what he would want, Lu?" From Deja.

"How you know he don't need us, Deja?" I fired back.

"He don't need us. He a grown-up." From Lynn.

"That don't mean nothing. My dad needed me yesterday. My mother, too." My voice started chipping.

"Yeah, and I take care of my mother," Patty said. "And my aunt." Finally.

"I look out for mine, too," Ghost added.

"And my dad," from Sunny.

"Look, all I'm saying is we've worked all year. Killing ourselves out here, fighting for this day. And we supposed to just throw it all away?" Aaron threw his arms around, dramatic. "I'm the captain. I say no."

"I'm the captain too. And *I* say yes," I replied.

The back-and-forth continued, everyone chiming in with what they thought we should do, but I was sticking to my guns.

"What's going on?" Whit finally came back over to what had almost become a mosh pit.

"This fool trying to get us to quit!" Aaron barked.

"No, I'm not!" I piped up, but then caught myself. "I'm not. I just . . . I don't know. I just don't feel right. *This* just don't feel right."

Whit looked from Aaron to me. "Okay, so . . . what do you think feels right, Lu?" she asked.

I looked down, then thought about Coach, and looked up. Looked Whit straight in the eyes. And it was like she read my face or something, because before I even said anything she said it for me. "Oh. Lu. The hospital? No. I don't . . . I don't think that's a good idea." Whit's face looked like it went numb.

"What would Coach do for us?" I asked. "Seriously. What would he do if any of us was jammed up like this? He would be there, even if it meant he couldn't make it to the track, or he couldn't pick up people for his cab job."

"That's a fact," Ghost confirmed. "He'd do anything to make sure we were good."

"If we run and win, he'll be proud of us, and he'll know we're the best athletes. But I don't think that's what he cares about. If we show up for him when he needs us, he'll know we family." I paused, and suddenly things started making sense. "*We'll* know we family."

"Let's take a vote on it," Aaron snapped, still not convinced.

Whit sighed. "If you wanna go see Coach, and . . . forfeit the championship, put a hand up." Me, Sunny, Ghost, and Patty's hands flew up first. And most of the others followed. They went up slowly, but they went up. "Well." Whit palmed her head and exhaled a loud breath. "I guess that's it."

"I'm not going," Aaron suddenly said. "I'm running. Track is about *your* time. It ain't about nobody else. So y'all go ahead, and I'm going to beat my best time. That's why Coach made me captain. I'm here to burn."

People started leaving the track, but I stayed. I was his co-captain. And we needed to figure this out.

"Aaron."

"Go 'head. Bounce. You ain't got the heart to be a champion," he sneered. "After all that work you put in on those hurdles. It's a shame."

"Maybe I don't," I said. "Maybe you right." I ain't have nothing else to say. I knew what I wanted to do. What I needed to do. I knew how to see the thing down the line. Not what was in front of me. Not what was in the way. "Have a good race, dude." I turned around and headed off the track, but then doubled back. "By the way, just so you know, I was never trying to take your spot. I know you worked for it, and I'm sorry if you ever felt that way."

I walked back over to the stands, where everyone had already told their parents about what was happening. Whit was answering questions and had gone over to the officials to let them know that the Defenders were pulling out. My mother was still handing oranges out to everyone, and my father was talking to Chris's father. Sunny's father to Ghost's mom. Patty's mom to Skunk. Everyone shaking their heads. Everyone confused and concerned, scrambling.

"We gotta go," I interrupted my dad's conversation.

And all he said was, "I know."

Whit came running back over, and a few minutes later, we were all back in our cars—Ghost and his family split up and rode with several people because they don't have a car—and we were headed out of the park, down the boulevard again. This time toward the hospital.

It was a silent ride. My mom and dad in the front seat. Me in the back. All of us quiet. No radio. No talking. My mother kept turning around to see me. To check on me. To see if there were any cracks. But I knew there weren't. I was solid.

Dad whipped into the hospital parking lot, cars pulling in all around us. We all jumped out and ran to the double doors, which automatically opened. It was a stampede into the waiting room. A bunch of kids in track uniforms, with their parents and friends. All the other people waiting looked up at us like we were some kind of flash mob. Like we were about to break into a dance routine or something. And when Sunny pushed through the crowd, for a moment I thought he was going to suggest it.

"Everybody, this is Ms. Melinda," he said, talking about the lady at the front desk. "Ms. Melinda, these are the Defenders."

"Oh, um . . . hi, hello, *Defenders*," the lady, Ms. Melinda, said, freaked out. She turned back to Sunny. "All of y'all here to see your grandfather?"

"Melinda!" Ghost's mom pushed through, cutting Sunny off before he could answer.

"Hey, Terri!" Ms. Melinda was getting more and more confused. "I thought you were in the cafeteria today."

"No. Not today. It was my son's first championship track meet. But his coach is in here."

"What's the name?"

"Otis Brody. Brought a baby in for an asthma attack," she explained.

"Tyrone!" I called out from the crowd.

"Baby's name is Tyrone," Ghost's mom confirmed. The lady started clicking and clacking on her computer, but before she could tell us anything, another set of double doors opened, the ones that led back into the doctor spaces, and Patty's aunt came walking out with a doctor. She was stretching her arm, bending and unbending it and bending and unbending it like it was her first time ever using an elbow and she was trying to get used it.

"Whoa!" she blurted out, walking right into our mob. "What in the . . . why are y'all here? I was on my way to you!"

"Gramps!" Sunny gave the doctor a hug.

"Momly!" Patty gave her aunt a hug, and Momly was able to finally hug her back after her arm had been in a cast for weeks. Patty and Sunny both tried to explain everything that was happening. I tried to fill in the holes, but all of it was sounding like the way my mother describes my music.

"Okay, okay!" Sunny's grandfather called out, trying to settle us all down. "Everyone! My name is Dr. Lancaster."

"My gramps," Sunny tossed in, in case we missed it.

"Yes, Sunny's grandfather. I know who you all are looking for. And I'm going to go get him. Please just sit tight, and . . . yeah. I'll be right back."

There weren't enough seats for all of us, so we made sure my mom—who by the way everybody was congratulating on my new baby-sister-to-be—got to sit.

"We're naming her Light. I named her that," I told *everyone*.

"That's a cool name, Lu," Patty said, sitting next to Cotton. "You might actually end up being a pretty good big brother . . . dummy." Cotton popped her on the arm.

Ghost was at the vending machine with Patty's sister, Maddy, pushing quarters in, buying a bag of sunflower seeds.

"No shells on the floor, Cas," his mother said. Then she looked around at us all. "If I knew we were all gonna be here, I could've gotten everybody some proper meals," she told Patty's mom, Ms. Jones.

Sunny leaned against the wall.

"You good?" I asked him.

"Just scared," he replied.

I went over to him, put my hand on his shoulder. "Me too," I told him. "I'm scared too."

And right then, the double doors opened again. The main ones that led outside. It was Aaron. He showed up. No sweat. No wrinkle, which meant, no race.

Nobody said nothing. Not good or bad. He came in with his mom and leaned against the opposite wall. Looked right at me. I looked right at him. Nodded.

We were all there. All of us. Like one of my mother's weird fruit sculptures, pieces of melon and berries and kiwi and a bunch of different kinds of oranges, all made to look like a team. A family. But it was like the toothpick to hold us in place was on the other side of the double doors.

Which . . . opened, again. The important ones leading into where the medical things happen. And finally, this time it was Coach.

We all went nuts.

"Coach, is everything okay?"

"Coach, how's your son?"

"How's Tyrone?"

"Where's Mrs. Margo?"

He put his hands up. "He's fine, he's fine! Everybody's fine. It was rough for moment, but it looks like

Ty is gonna be okay. But . . . why aren't y'all on the track?" Coach checked his watch, balled his face up.

And we all went silent. It was like all the sound in the room had been sucked out. You couldn't even hear the clicks of Ms. Melinda's keyboard no more.

Ghost gave me a look. Sunny, a chin up. Patty straight-up dug her elbow into my side. And from Aaron? A nod. I looked at the floor for a second. Then looked up at Coach waiting. *Lead with the knee.* I stepped forward. Cleared my throat.

"Well . . . see . . . we—"

"Ahyoo!" Ghost fake-coughed, doing a terrible job at masking the fact that he was saying, *you.* As in, *me.*

"*I* . . . was feeling so . . . so, bad. We all were. But . . . I . . ."

"Just say it, Lu!" From Patty. Coach glanced at her, then back at me. Tilted his head, turned his eyes from circles to lines. I nodded, swallowed.

"Coach, I . . . I suggested we . . . um . . . we forfeit the championship."

"For me?" he looked confused and honestly, a little mad. "Why would you . . . You all were fully prepared to run it without me. Y'all were ready."

I looked around at my friends, my teammates, and everyone looked like they were waiting for me to explain, but I couldn't find the right words. How do you explain something that's just a feeling on the inside? Lightning in my gut?

"Coach, um, yesterday I learned a new word," I started, trying to figure out how to make it make sense. "Integrity. You know what that means?" Coach raised an eyebrow, crossed his arms. "Well, if you don't, it means basically having a gold medal . . . on the inside."

"Does that mean you have to—" Sunny piped up, but was cut off.

"Sunny." Dr. Lancaster used one finger to shush him, and his other hand to pat Sunny's back.

"A gold medal on the inside, huh?" Coach said, now stepping toward me. "And where you learn that?"

"From, uh, my dad," I said. And as Coach cut his eyes toward my dad, I continued, "From you."

Coach's arms dropped. Fell to his sides, loose but heavy.

"And all y'all good with this?" Coach asked, now looking around the room. Everyone nodded, some fast, some slow, some barely. Aaron's was almost invisible and might've been a single nod. But they all nodded.

Coach got right up on me. Tilted his head to the right. Then to the left. Studying me. Looking for cracks. Then he smiled small. Nodded. "Okay. Okay, okay, well, I was going to surprise you all with something after the championship. But since, apparently, this *is* the championship, I guess I'll give it to you now." Coach stepped back. "Everybody line up."

Huh? But we all maneuvered around the room side by side, lining the walls, going around our friends and families and other people who were sick, waiting to be called, watching us like some kind of stage play. On my right was Sunny, Patty, Ghost, and on my left, the last person in line—Aaron.

Coach reached in his back pocket, pulled out the medal.

The

Olympic

Gold

Medal.

You would've thought he pulled a sword out his back pocket the way people flipped out, and I couldn't blame them. It was as if he was holding a star in the palm of his hand.

"You really *were* in the Olympics, Coach?" Deja asked.

"I knew it!" Krystal said.

Mikey smiled. With teeth.

Sunny teared up.

But something was different about the medal. It was just the gold plate. No ribbon to hang it around your neck, which is the best part, if you ask me. The best necklace in the world.

"This is my medal. I won this thing about twenty years ago, and it was like lightning struck me. I never felt so electric. It was the greatest day of my life, until Tyrone was born. But I lost this medal for a long time, and recently, lightning struck twice, a friend of mine, um . . . yeah . . . a friend of mine found it for me. And when he brought it to me, I realized something. I realized what I hope some of y'all realized this year. When I lost this medal, I didn't really lose anything but a piece of gold. A symbol to remind me of my hard work. But I never needed to be reminded of that. When I got this medal back, it came with so much more. A different reminder. A reminder of the friends and family I made on that track putting in all that hard work. The help-ups, the cheers, the pushing, and pulling. Sharing the load. Finding a new kind of freedom. Being a better version of myself every day." Then Coach dropped his head. "But I'm not perfect."

"Head up, Coach!" Ghost ordered. Coach picked it up. His eyes were watering.

"I'm, um . . . I'm not perfect," he repeated, now

wiping away a tear. "But none of us are. And what we learn is that if we push, if we aren't scared to be scared, if we're not terrified of being uncomfortable, if we can trust ourselves and be honest about where we fall short, where we miss the bar, and can accept a little help, which we all need sometimes, we can be . . . good."

"We can be great," Aaron spoke up. And it didn't sound like a suck-up.

"Yeah," Coach sniffled. "Yeah. Okay . . . that's enough of that." He tried to pull himself together. Took some deep breaths, wiped his face. "So, to finally celebrate you all . . ." Coach reached in his other back pocket and pulled out a bunch of fabric that was all paper-clipped together. He slid the clip off and held the bunch of purple squares in the air. "This was—is—my Olympic ribbon. I cut it up this morning. I want each of you to take a piece and pass the bunch to the person next to you so that they can take a piece. Right now, we get to decide what this—this first-place ribbon—is to us. We get to name ourselves. Some people call us a team. Defenders. Some say we're just knucklehead kids and a cab-driving coach. I call us family." More sniffles, as he handed the pieces of ribbon to Whit. Whit took a square off the top, passed them to Krystal. Krystal took one, passed them to Deja. Deja took one and passed them to Chris. Chris to Brit-Brat. Brit-Brat to Mikey. And on and on and on and on until Curron passed them to Ghost.

Five left.

Five of us left.

Ghost took a piece. Passed them to Patty.

Patty took a piece. Passed them to Sunny.

Sunny took a piece. Passed them to me.

And I took my piece, and put the last piece in Aaron's hand.

He closed his fingers around mine and said, "Thank you . . . Captain."

I nodded, replied, "All good, bro."

All good.

ACKNOWLEDGMENTS

Well, we've come to the end of what, for me, has been an incredible journey. There are so many people to thank. First and foremost, my editor, Caitlyn Dlouhy, and agent Elena Giovinazzo. Also, Holly McGhee, who was there at the conception of this series. I'm grateful to my childhood friends, to the real Ghost, Patina, Sunny, and Lu. To the real Aaron, Mikey, and Curron. To the real Krystal, Deja, and Brit-Brat. To the real Coach Brody. I owe you all and am grateful for the impact you all have had on my life. A special thank-you to Michael Posey, for helping out with the details of the sport. A huge thank-you to Vanessa Brantley-Newton for nailing the jacket art. I think they're absolutely perfect, and (hopefully) will stand the test of time. And most importantly, thank you to the readers. To everyone who has run these races. To every "This is the first book I've ever read, cover to cover." To every "What?? How you just gonna end it like that?" To every "I've never seen myself in a book before." I love you. And know, you've changed my life.

Remember, tuck your elbows, open your stride, breathe, breathe, breathe.

I'll see you at the finish line,

Jason

BY
JASON REYNOLDS

Discussion Questions

1. In literature, a symbol is something that
    represents a bigger idea. In this book, nicknames
    are often used symbolically. Explain how the
    symbol of a lightning bolt applies to Lu. What
    characteristics do they share? How does the
    symbol of a wolf apply to Torrie Cunningham?
    If you were going to choose a symbol to repre-
    sent yourself, what would you choose? Explain
    your answer. Think about other symbols in the
    book, like hurdles, light, and shields. How does
    Jason Reynolds use these symbols to express
    larger ideas or themes?

2. How can you tell that Lu has conflicting feelings about becoming a big brother? Can you
describe his emotions after his parents' surprise announcement? Have you ever been
happy and upset about something at the same
time? Do you think Lu is going to be a good
big brother? Explain your answer.

3. Why is Lu hesitant to jump hurdles in practice? Has being nervous or afraid ever kept
you from trying something?

4. Why do you think Coach points Lu toward
Torrie Cunningham? What lesson does he
hope Lu will take away from this interaction?
Look at the way Reynolds describes Torrie.
What do these descriptions tell you about
how drugs have affected Torrie's life?

5. Lu jokes that he is "'the fine-o albino.'" What
does it mean to be albino? What causes
albinism? How rare is it in humans and other
species? How does being albino affect Lu?
Consider both physical and emotional effects.

6. In this novel, Lu and his teammates tease each other playfully, but several of the characters deal with the lingering effects of bullying. Is there a difference between talking trash, or roasting, and bullying? For example, do you think Patty bullies Shante Morris? Do you think Shante Morris is a bully? Do you think people who tease others understand the impact of their words?

7. How does Lu's father know Coach Otis? How did Otis's teasing affect Lu's father when they were teenagers? Do you think Otis knew how hurtful his words were? Explain your answer.

8. What do you think it means to be cool? Do you think different people will have different answers to that question? What decisions did Lu's father make when he was trying to be cool? How can you tell that he regrets these decisions?

9. One of the things Lu and his mother disagree on is their taste in music. What compromise

do they work out? Do you know which musicians or songs your parents listened to when they were young? What do you think about their favorite music? What do they think about the music you like?

10. Who is Kelvin Jefferson? How did he influence Lu's decision to start running track? Why is Lu scared when he sees him again? Why didn't he tell anyone, including his friend Ghost, about being bullied? Do you think he should have? How might the situation have turned out differently if he had?

11. How would you define irony? Several situations in this book are good examples of irony. Identify one and explain why it can be considered ironic.

12. Why do you think Lu is able to jump the hurdles when he is not wearing contacts? Are you ever tempted to focus on the obstacles ahead instead of your end goal? What lesson can you take from Reynolds's book about facing and overcoming challenges?

13. When Lu delivers the fruit sculpture to Maria Gonzales at the Sword and the Stone, what does she tell him about the legend of King Arthur? What does thinking about this legend help Lu realize about himself?

14. How does Lu find out that his dad has Coach's gold medal? What happens when he confronts his father about it? Have you ever had to confront an adult? What happened?

15. How did Lu's father end up with the gold medal? Why do you think it takes him so long to return it? Lu witnesses the conversation between his father and Coach from a distance, but does not hear what each man says. What do you think they said to each other? Do you think they're both at fault in this situation?

16. Why do you think Lu's dad takes Lu with him when he confronts Wolf? Do you think this changes the way Lu views his father?

17. The word *sympathy* means the ability to feel another person's feelings, but the word

empathy is a bit different. Having empathy means you are able to understand why another person feels or acts the way they do. Though Lu does not agree with what his father or Kelvin Jefferson have done, he displays empathy toward them. Explain the series of realizations that help him develop this empathy. Studies have shown that reading fiction helps develop empathy. How has this book helped you to understand other people? Which character do you most identify with? Explain your answer.

18. Lu spends time reflecting on the word *integrity*. How do his actions at the end of the book demonstrate integrity? How important is integrity to you? Can you name a choice you've made that was influenced by your sense of integrity?

19. At the championship meet, what decision do the Defenders make as a team? Would you have made the same decision if you had been on this team? Explain your answer.

20. Have you read any of the other books in Reynolds's Track series? If so, how did this book increase your understanding of the characters? If not, is there another member of the Defenders whom you would like to learn more about?

Guide prepared by Amy Jurskis, English Department Chair at Oxbridge Academy.

This guide has been provided by Simon & Schuster for classroom, library, and reading group use. It may be reproduced in its entirety or excerpted for these purposes.

TURN THE PAGE FOR A PEEK AT
ANOTHER JASON REYNOLDS BOOK:
AS BRAVE AS YOU

#460: POOP. POOP iS STUPiD. STUPiD POOP. STUPiD. POOPiD. POOPiDiTY. IS POOPiDiTY a WORD?

Genie stood a few feet away from Samantha's shabby old doghouse, scribbling a mess of words in his notebook. His older brother, Ernie, was luring the mutt to a cleaner spot in the yard with a big pot of leftover chicken, bacon, grits, greens, and whatever else was for doggy breakfast.

"Okay, that should keep her busy for a few minutes," Ernie said, successful. He walked over to the side of Grandma and Grandpop's house, grabbed a rusty shovel, then came back to Genie and started scooping up crusty piles of dog poop.

"What I wanna know is what you 'bout to do with that mess?" Genie asked, pinching and pulling his shorts out of his butt. Ma must not have noticed how much he had grown since the year before when she packed all his old summer clothes.

"If you put that notebook down, you'll see," Ernie said, holding the shovel out and walking toward the back of the house where all the trees were. When he got close enough to the wood line, he looked over his shoulder. Genie shoved the small notebook into his back pocket. "You watchin'?" Ernie called out, making sure all eyes were on him.

Genie hustled over. "Yeah." Ernie flashed a sly grin, one that worked perfectly with his dark shades. Then, without giving any kind of warning, he cocked the shovel back and flung it forward. The poop flew into the air and out into the woods, slapping against the trees and exploding.

"Ooh yeah!" Ernie cheered, holding his shovel up as if he had just scored a touchdown.

Genie gaped, his mouth falling open as Ernie came back to scoop up more dog crud. "You just gon' stand there, or you gon' get in on this?" Ernie asked, chin-pointing to the other shovel leaning against the side of the house.

No way was Genie going to miss out on slinging poop. On *poopidity*? No. Way. How often does anybody get to catapult doo-doo into a forest? Never. Genie ran and grabbed the other shovel.

"Get this one," Ernie said, stabbing at a gross mound, still stinky.

Genie grimaced, but he slid the shovel under the poop, grimaced again at the scratchy sound of metal on dirt, then lifted it and followed Ernie back to the tree line.

"Go for it," Ernie said, nodding.

Genie put one foot forward, holding the shovel as if it were a baseball bat and he was about to attempt the worst bunt in history. He whipped the shovel forward, but not nearly hard enough. The poop plopped down only about a foot away. It was a pretty sad throw, and it was way too close to being a situation where poop was splattered all over Genie's Converses. Yeah, they were already covered in dust, but dust is one thing, even mud he could handle, but dog poop? There's no coming back from that.

"You gotta *fling* it, Genie. *Fling* it." Ernie demonstrated with a few ghost flings. "You see that tree over there?"

Genie looked out at all the trees in front of

them and wondered which one Ernie was talking about. It was pretty much . . . a forest. Trees were everywhere. And Ernie wasn't really pointing at any one in particular. He just said *that tree over there* as if one of the trees had been marked with a sign that said THIS TREE, DUMMY. But Ernie was always on him about asking too many questions, so Genie just nodded.

"Watch and learn, young grasshoppa." Ernie held the shovel low, letting it hang behind him before hurling its contents into the woods. It splat against a tree. Perfect shot. It must've been the one Ernie was aiming for, because he threw his hands up in celebration again. "Bang, bang! Got it!" he howled. "Now, try again."

Genie picked up another clump, questions flying all over the place like those flies on the . . . poopidity. Why was there so much of it in the first place? Did nobody else care that there was mess all over the yard? When was the last time the yard had been poop-scooped? Genie tried to mimic Ernie's every move. He held the shovel low and let it drop back behind him a little so that he could get some good momentum. We're talking technique here. Sophisticated stuff.

"Aim for that old house back there," Ernie said, pointing into the woods. Genie focused and counted off. One, two, and on three, he swung his whole body, a kind of broke-down golf swing, the mess whipping from the shovel head. Genie definitely got some air on it this time! But he hadn't quite figured out how to aim it—Ernie left that part out. The poop zipped off behind him, slamming into a window in the back of the house. The *wrong* house. His grandparents' house.

"Genie!" Ernie shouted, his eyes bugging. And right after that came Grandma.

"Genie!" she called out. "Ernie! What in Sam Hill are y'all doin'?"

Grandma was the one who put Ernie and Genie on poop patrol in the first place, in case you were wondering. Neither one of them had ever had to shovel poop out of anybody's yard before, because first of all, in Brooklyn, most people don't have yards. And secondly, most Brooklyn folks just pick it up with plastic Baggies whenever a dog does his doo on the sidewalk. Not everybody, but the majority. But there were no sidewalks here in North Hill, Virginia. No brownstones with the cement stoops where you could watch the buses, ice cream trucks, and taxis ride by. Nope. North Hill, Virginia, was country. Like *country* country. And Genie and Ernie were staying there in a small white house on the top of a hill. Grandma and Grandpop's house. For a month. Like thirty *whole* days.